He turned to look at her. A hot jolt of electric current shot between them.

Brice stopped walking. His eyes grazed her face like a tender caress. Naomi felt a pulse begin to beat between her thighs. Her heart felt as if it was tumbling around in her chest as she watched his face come closer to hers until his image blurred and his warm lips brushed against her own.

He groaned deep in his throat as her lips parted ever so slightly and she allowed him to run the tip of his tongue across the inside of her mouth.

Naomi felt weak all over, yet her body was on fire. This wasn't her. This wasn't what she did with virtual strangers. But she couldn't help herself. She couldn't stop and she didn't want to. When his fingers pressed into her back and brought her closer, her own sighs floated into the night sky as she felt the weight of his sex press against her.

If she would have only one night with Brice Lawrence, she was going to take it.

Books by Donna Hill

Kimani Romance

Love Becomes Her
If I Were Your Woman
After Dark
Sex and Lies
Seduction and Lies
Temptation and Lies
Longing and Lies
Private Lessons

DONNA HILL

began writing novels in 1990. Since that time she has had more than forty titles published, including full-length novels and novellas. Two of her novels and one novella were adapted for television. She has won numerous awards for her body of work. She is also the editor of five novels, two of which were nominated for awards. She easily moves from romance to erotica, horror, comedy and women's fiction. She was the first recipient of the Trailblazer Award and currently teaches writing at the Frederick Douglass Creative Arts Center.

Donna lives in Brooklyn with her family. Visit her Web site at www.donnahill.com.

Private LESSONS
Donna Hill

KIMANI
ROMANCE

This book is dedicated to the countless men and women
who have devoted their lives to education.

KIMANI PRESS™

ISBN-13: 978-0-373-86176-7

Recycling programs
for this product may
not exist in your area.

PRIVATE LESSONS

Dear Reader,

Thank you for once again entrusting me to take you on a romantic journey. I do hope you will be intrigued by my brainy, beautiful heroine, Naomi Clarke, a tenured professor, and Brice Lawrence, the man who makes her forget her lesson plans!

When these two meet for the first time on the balmy beaches of the Bahamas, neither suspects that their little vacation fling will not only put them together in bed, but…well, you'll have to find out for yourself.

Do let me know what you think. I'd love to hear from you. Drop me a line at dhassistant@gmail.com.

Until next time,

Donna

Chapter 1

"Come on, Naomi, live a little," Alexis said as they browsed the swimsuit selections in the Neiman Marcus department store. "Go for a bikini." She held up a fire-engine-red two-piece that was really no more than a few strings knotted together.

"You have got to be kidding!" Naomi sputtered, shoving the strings back at Alexis.

Alexis couldn't contain her laughter. "Girl, relax. I know that's not your style, but we're going on vacation. We won't know a soul. It wouldn't hurt for you to let that bun down and flaunt yourself a little bit. Maybe catch the eye of some fine island man." She winked. "'Cause that's what I plan to do." She rifled through the swimsuit rack.

"So I guess it's over between you and Gary."

Alexis waved her hand in dismissal. "Gary was much too boring. All he ever wanted to do was watch CNN. Can you imagine?"

"What's wrong with that? At least you know where he is and what he's doing," she said, her tone dipping down to that place she didn't want to go.

Alexis sighed and turned to her friend. She knew all too well where the bitterness stemmed from. "Nay, what Trevor did to you was despicable. And I hope he rots in hell for hurting you the way what he did. But it's been two years." She paused and took Naomi by the shoulders. "You need to let it go so that you can be okay, sweetie. All you do is work and you need more than that. Your life can be more than your students and grading papers and going to meetings."

Naomi pressed her lips together and looked at her friend. Alexis's soft features and inviting brown eyes were the pictures of concern. She knew Alexis was right. But she wasn't like Alexis. She couldn't bounce from one man to the next. She'd always been reserved and shy when it came to relationships. Sure, she'd enjoyed the attention of men just like any other heterosexual woman, but her conservative nature never really allowed her to "let go." Although she'd always been a workaholic and driven, and not the party type, when she'd met Trevor, a professor at Morehouse University during an educator's conference in D.C., a lot of that changed. He wooed her into opening that door that she'd always kept shut. She'd stepped out from behind her books and research papers to become a partner in a relationship. What a mistake. So when it was over she did what was familiar and comfortable: she buried herself in her work, only deeper this time.

Naomi's expression eased. She shook off the images of the past with a toss of her head. "I let you talk me into this trip, didn't I?" she teased, moving out of Alexis's hold as she reached for a swimsuit. She held up a one-piece lemon yellow suit with cut-outs on the sides. She smiled triumphantly.

Alexis angled her head left then right. "Hmm. Okay. Not bad. Kinda cute."

"Gee thanks." She laughed lightly. Two years is a long time to be alone, she silently admitted as they continued shopping. But she'd rather be alone than to be hurt like that again. She was going on this trip because Alexis had all but twisted her arm and her relentless badgering finally broke her down. Hmm, two weeks on a sunny island was probably what she needed.

By the time Naomi returned home from their all-out shopping spree, her feet were on fire. She kicked off her shoes and her feet sighed in contentment. She flexed her toes. Alexis must have dragged her to every outlet in the mall—twice. She laughed lightly thinking about her friend. Alexis

Montgomery was a piece of work, but she wouldn't trade her in for anything.

Naomi went upstairs to her bedroom. She loved her bedroom. It was her haven and she'd taken special care in decorating it. When she walked into her bedroom all the rest of the world disappeared.

The walls were a soft cream color and in opposite corners were floor to ceiling curios lined with first edition books. The bay window opened onto her backyard below and the garden that she tended with care. The cool walls held several pieces of African art that she'd purchased from a small gallery in Sag Harbor. The inlaid wood floors were only partially covered by an antique rug in cream and bronze.

But her bed was her centerpiece. Queen-size, four-poster with sheer draping that hung dramatically from the tops of the posts. She'd spent a fortune on her mattress that was like lying down in heaven. A matching six-dresser drawer, a double door armoire and a cozy club chair rounded out the furnishings. Small speakers were tucked into strategic spots to pipe in her music when the mood hit her. Recessed lighting offered the perfect ambiance for any time of the day or night. Plants, rather than drapes, hung in abundance in her windows, giving the room a sometimes tropical, but calming feel.

Naomi drew in a long breath of satisfaction and began to feel the aura of her room begin to work its magic. She dumped the bags on the bed and started unpacking them. As she viewed the brightly colored outfits, the strappy sandals and glittery jewelry and even a few purchases from Victoria's Secret, she grew more and more pleased and excited. A bubble of anticipation fluttered in her stomach, and she knew that with Alexis she was going to have a great time, like it or not!

She began taking tags off and sorting through the clothing when she noticed the flashing light on her phone. She walked around the queen-size bed to the end table and pressed the flashing message light.

The first call was obviously a wrong number as the caller was talking in a completely different language. The next was from her mortgage company reminding her that she was eligible for refinancing. The next call stopped her cold.

"Naomi. It's Trevor. I—"

She pressed Erase before she could hear another word. This was the third call from him in the past month and she'd erased all the other calls as well. How dare he, she fumed. She should have changed her number when they broke up but she never expected to hear from him again. She hadn't said anything to Alexis about the calls. But she definitely planned to talk with her about it while they were away—get her perspective.

She pressed the heel of her palm to her forehead and turned in a slow circle of frustration. She felt violated in a way, as crazy as that might sound. But his call invaded her one sanctuary.

"Aggggh!" She stomped over to her walk-in closet,

pulled out her suitcase and began packing her clothes. At that moment she wished she was on her way to the airport, instead of the coming weekend. She shoved the clothes in the bag.

Yes, a trip with her best friend for two carefree weeks in Antigua was exactly what she needed.

Trevor Lloyd was more than a little disappointed that he'd been, once again, unable to reach Naomi. He'd tried several times by phone, left messages and she hadn't returned any of his calls.

He got up from the brown second-hand couch and walked to the window. The sun was beginning to set and in this muted light the blight on this urban neighbourhood was dulled. A far cry from the five bedroom, two-story Tudor he once owned.

Trevor shoved his hands into the pockets of his hand-tailored slacks—one of the few things he hadn't given up from his old life. He drew in a long breath.

How had he gotten here—two steps above bottom? He'd been a respected professor, an upstanding member of his community, a sought-out lecturer, financially secure and he'd had someone who'd loved him.

He turned away from the telltale reflection in the window. It was all gone now and he had no one to blame but himself. But he was back and determined to reclaim his place on all fronts and in Naomi Clarke's heart.

* * *

"Can I refill your drink, ma'am?"

Naomi peered above her dark sunglasses. A waiter stood above her balancing a silver-toned tray on his palm, his dark, shiny face in sharp contrast to his brilliant white jacket. She glanced to her right side. Her daiquiri glass was empty. She lifted it and pushed it toward the waiter. "Thank you, yes."

"Virgin again, ma'am?" he asked with a smile that Naomi translated as condescending.

Her gaze faltered. Her full, glossy lips pinched ever so slightly. "Yes," she murmured, and pushed her sunglasses back up along the bridge of her pert nose.

She adjusted her sheer tangerine-colored wrap across her lap and folded her long fingers on top. *Did he have to say "virgin" so loud?*

She shifted her body on the blue-and-white-striped lounge chair and crossed her ankles. She glanced toward the pool—and when she drew in a breath of sheer shock and pleasure, all the air stuck in the center of her chest. He emerged from the pool and pushed up onto the deck, the muscles in his arms bulging and glistening. The water clung to him as if it didn't want to let him go, even as he took a towel and wiped the droplets from his face and broad shoulders.

Naomi commanded herself to breathe before her head started to spin from lack of oxygen.

Brice couldn't believe his luck. It was her.

Stretched out like a Nubian goddess. He'd noticed her when she'd arrived at the hotel the prior afternoon. Then, she was disguised in a two-piece skirt suit. Her dark black hair was pulled back into a bun at the nape of her neck, forcing her cheekbones to stand out against her warm brown complexion, and giving her expression an exotic appearance.

She'd crossed the lobby with the assurance of someone used to exerting her authority, and walked directly to the check-in desk. Alone. He'd looked for her later that evening in the lobby, the bar, the restaurant and even out on the beach. It was almost as if he'd imagined her. Until now.

He draped his towel around his neck. This time he wasn't going to let her get away. He started off in her direction, but slowed when he watched the exchange between her and the waiter. She practically shoved the glass at him, and the tight purse of her lips didn't invite conversation. Maybe he needed to set his sights elsewhere, after all. He walked toward the bar instead.

Naomi watched him change directions and her heart sunk. She was sure that the gorgeous man that she'd noticed since yesterday was actually heading in her way. Wishful thinking. Even if he did decide to introduce himself, she'd probably make a mess of it. Relationships weren't her strong suit. She was an academic, a nerd, a brainiac, a one-time child prodigy turned genius, with a doctorate and two master's degrees. Whose favorite pastime was reading a good book. Her intellect generally put most men off, which effectively limited her dating prospects.

Getting away and taking a vacation far from her normal life was her best friend Alexis's idea. They were supposed to travel together, but at the last minute Alexis had to cancel, due to her mother's illness. So here she was, alone, like a fish out of water and not a clue what to do next. If she wasn't as passionate about money as she was about books, she would have cancelled the trip. But the "no refund" policy stopped her cold.

"Your drink, ma'am."

The condescending waiter was back. "Thank you," she murmured.

He gave a slight nod of his bald, shiny head and walked away.

Naomi took off her sunglasses and set them on the table next to her and picked up her drink and sipped from the straw. She took a long, slow look around her.

Everywhere that she turned people were having a ball. Couples toyed with and teased each other, small groups held impromptu parties and stray singles seemed to quickly find a partner.

Her brows pulled together. Why was this so difficult for her? Why was it always so hard for her to loosen up, relax and enjoy herself?

The truth was, she'd never had time. From the time her parents realized that they had a baby genius, they scraped and saved to put her in every kind of class they could afford: piano, violin, dance, math, science. But then her father had a heart attack when she was fifteen, and he was totally incapacitated. Naomi's classes came to a grinding halt. She took on a job after school, took care of her younger brother, Paul, and helped her mother around the house. Her entertainment became the world of books.

When it was time for college, Naomi put that out of her head. It wasn't an option for her. Her parents had exhausted their savings taking care of her father, and she was vehement about not leaving them, even when her parents insisted that she go. It was her guidance counselor, Ms. Adams, who convinced Naomi that to waste her intelligence would be a crying shame. Throughout her high school years, she'd been more than a stellar student and was slated to be valedictorian, graduating a year early.

She would be the first in her family to go to college, Ms. Adams had insisted. Don't waste your gift, she'd urged. After much cajoling and insistence from her parents, Naomi let go of the reins on her dreams and with Ms. Adams's help began filling out applications. By the time she was halfway through her senior year, she had her pick of universities and the scholarship money she'd needed.

Naomi chose Spelman so that she could stay close to home. Then she was admitted to Columbia University in New York for her two graduate degrees in English and Contemporary Literature and her doctorate in African-American Studies.

Now, at thirty-four, she was a tenured professor at Atlanta College, on track to become dean. She had a house, a car, a fulfilling career—but, as Billy Dee William said in *Mahogany,* it's nothing without someone to share it with.

"Are the drinks that bad?"

Naomi blinked and looked up, shielding her eyes from the glare of the sun with the curve of her hand. It was him!

She nearly spilled her drink.

She ran her tongue across her lips. Brice tracked the sensual movement and wondered if it was as sweet as it looked.

"I…I don't know what you mean," she finally managed to say.

"You're frowning. Is the drink that bad," he repeated.

The sun blazed behind him, casting him in a magnificent glow that created an almost surreal image.

"Oh." Her light laugh fluttered and stumbled in her throat. "Just thinking."

"Antigua isn't the place for deep thoughts. Mind if I sit down?" He indicated the empty chair beside her with a lift of his chin.

"I'm sure it's fine." *Don't act too eager. Play it cool.*

He lowered his long, lean body onto the chair and stretched out. Naomi tried to swallow over the hard, dry knot that rose in her throat as she glanced

down at the bulge in his swim trunks and the tight
muscular thighs. A line of perspiration broke out
along her hairline. She uncrossed and recrossed her
legs. *Breathe.*

"As I was saying, Antigua isn't a place for deep
thought. You're supposed to be having fun." He
turned his head to look at her and immediately had to
order his body to back down and stay under control.
He dropped his towel across his lap.

Up close, she was more tantalizing than he'd first
thought. The warm brown of her skin, tinted by the
rays of the sun, was as appealing as an appetizer
before the main course. Her face looked as if it had
been carved by a sculptor's expert hand: wide, dark
eyes, prominent cheekbones reminiscent of the
ancestors, and silky black hair. Her long neck led
down to the rise of heaven. Her breasts were perfect,
full and round, not too much, and not too little,
her chest tapering down to tight abs, all balanced
on dancer's legs. Her body could put the *Sports
Illustrated* swimsuit cover model to shame. That
dowdy outfit she had on the day before definitely
hid her assets. This was one hot sister, from the top
of her beautiful head down to the tips of her pink-
polished toes.

Naomi was amazed at the length of his lashes and
how they framed his dark eyes, the smoothness of his
milk chocolate skin and full lips that seemed eager to
offer a smile or a sensual kiss. She forced her mind

away from his mouth and what he hid beneath the towel.

"What makes you think I'm not having fun?" she asked, bringing them both crashing back to reality.

His eyes glided slowly across her face. A hint of a smile curved his mouth. "*Are* you?"

Her gaze was glued to his lips when he spoke, tracing the outline of them, their fullness and the way they matched perfectly with the hard lines of his face.

The raucous laughter of a group of partygoers passing in front of them snapped her back to attention.

"I'm having a ball." She put the straw between her lips and sucked deeply.

He chuckled. "My name is Brice."

His voice was like a gentle rumble before a storm, she thought.

"Naomi."

"Pleasure to meet you, Naomi."

Her heart was pounding so furiously at this point, that she was certain he could hear it.

"Are you here with friends?"

If she said no, would that paint her as desperate, she worried. But if she said yes, where would she drum up these "friends?"

"I'm on vacation," she managed to finally shoot out.

Brice knew a cold shoulder when he felt one. It was obviously a mistake. He should have listened to his gut in the first place and stayed away. He pushed up from his seat. "Well, enjoy your vacation, Naomi."

Before she could think of anything to say to stop him, he was walking away. Naomi slumped back against the chair and sighed. *That went swimmingly*, she thought, her spirits sinking. She may as well paint a note on her forehead saying "stay away."

She reached for her sunglasses and put them back on to hide the disappointment in her eyes. This was only her first day and she was turning men away already. She had nine more to go. Would the rest of her time in paradise be just as miserable?

Brice stole a parting glance at Naomi from across his left shoulder. *That was a mistake,* he thought, while he watched her return to her haughty pose, throwing up the barrier and her dark glasses. He shook his head and strode toward the hotel lobby, then took the elevator to his room. He had no one but himself to blame for the annoyance he felt. But he could certainly blame Naomi for the uncomfortable tightness in his groin. He should have paid attention to his gut instinct and kept his distance from the ice queen. There were plenty of lovely, available women on the island who would welcome his company. But the truth was, he'd been on the island for a week and not one of these bathing beauties had caught his eye. Until Naomi. He wasn't the type of guy to be so easily dissuaded. His philosophy had always been "only take no for an answer when you have exhausted all possibilities." He hadn't even put up the good fight yet. He smiled to himself. *Ms. Naomi, I'm going turn that ice into liquid fire.*

Chapter 2

"So tell me, tell me. How was your first day?" Alexis asked.

"Before we get to me, how is your mom?"

Alexis blew out a sigh. "She's doing better. But she really put a scare into me this time. COPD is no joke but she refuses to stop smoking. Just makes me crazy. They had to intubate her this time to get her lungs working. Girl, it was crazy. She should be coming home by the end of the week. I'm getting a home attendant for her. Hopefully, they can keep an eye on her."

Naomi harrumphed. Alexis's mother, Sylvia, was a chronic smoker and over the past few years it had begun to really take its toll. This wasn't her first trip to the hospital and if she didn't do something about her habit, it wouldn't be the last. She worried about Sylvia, and particularly about Alexis. As much as Alexis may fuss about her mother, she adored her. Sylvia had been a single mom who sacrificed to make sure that Alexis had whatever she needed and Alexis never forgot that.

"Well, you just tell her to behave herself and that I'm thinking of her."

"I will. So, now back to you. How is it going?"

Naomi hugged the phone between her cheek and shoulder while she took off her sandals and put them in the closet. "Could be worse, I suppose."

"Oh, Nay, what happened? You didn't introduce yourself as doctor and act like your usual self did you?"

"What's that supposed to mean?" She smoothed the bedcovering and sat down.

"You know exactly what I mean. Distant and above it all."

"You're wrong for that, Lexi," she said, feigning hurt.

"Did you at least try to meet anyone?"

She thought about the gorgeous man named Brice who kept invading her thoughts and then her space, and what a disaster that turned out to be. Finally, she spilled it all to Alexis. She could almost see her friend shaking her head with disappointment.

"Girl, what am I going to do with you? Don't you remember anything that I told you?"

Naomi sighed. "Lexi it's useless. I'm not like you. I'm not a party girl. I'd just as soon teach my class naked than flirt with a perfect stranger."

Alexis moaned. Naomi Clarke was clearly the African-American version of Dr. Brennan on the television show *Bones*. They were both unbelievably brilliant, beautiful and totally naive about the ways of the regular world. Rather than give in to feelings, they would prefer to rationalize everything away. It was both endearing and frustrating.

She'd lost count of the number of times that she set Naomi up with a date that Nay turned into an inquisition or a telethon about the state of the world, people, politics, religion, education. You name it and Naomi Clarke could talk to you about it. On and on and on. Besides her bedazzling the men with her sheer volume of knowledge, Naomi had this standoffish air about her.

The sad part was, she was the complete opposite once you got to know her. But she rarely gave anyone the chance. The only man who could even come close to holding a conversation with her were some of the other professors on campus. But that relationship choice was a definite no-no to the college administration.

"Nay, do me one favor?"

"What?" she asked halfheartedly.

"Why don't you spend the rest of the week pretending to be someone completely different?"

"I don't know what you're talking about."

Alexis groaned. "Playacting. Role playing. Didn't you ever play 'pretend' when you were a kid?"

Naomi frowned in concentration. "No. I don't think so."

If this was anyone other than Naomi, Alexis would swear that she was lying. "Listen, this is what I want you to do…"

Naomi took her time dressing for dinner. She'd spent most of the afternoon sitting on the balcony of her room, rereading *Invisible Man* by Ralph Ellison, and watching with envy the lighthearted frivolity on the beach below. Why she couldn't unwind she wondered for the umpteenth time. She didn't "party" as Alexis would say, although that girl made it a point to hook her up with every eligible bachelor she could find, and drag her to every night spot in Atlanta that played music, served drinks and had men. Those were Alexis's only criteria.

But Naomi wanted more than a good-time man. She wanted someone with a brain, ambition. Someone who didn't care that she didn't know the latest hit on the radio or that she loved movies with subtitles—and spent Saturday afternoons following new Thai, Japanese or African recipes or rereading books that she loved. And he wouldn't care that she was probably the only black woman in Atlanta with no rhythm. None of those things would matter, because he would simply adore her for who she was, quirks and all.

She peered into the mirror of the dressing table and applied a light covering of lip gloss. Maybe she should take Alexis's advice, she briefly mused. Sighing, she placed the tube on the dresser top and stared at her reflection. She could almost see Alexis sitting on her shoulder, and she could hear her whispering, "live a little."

Naomi drew in a long breath of resolve, squared her shoulders and unbuttoned the top two buttons of her sleeveless cotton blouse, exposing a lush hint of cleavage. Frowning, she quickly fastened one button, picked up her purse and headed out for the evening, intent on enjoying herself, one way or the other. And if Brice should just so happen to give her another chance, she was going to take it!

Brice was seated at the outdoor bar adjacent to the beachfront restaurant when he caught a flash of something soft and flowing in his peripheral vision. He turned in the direction of the movement and a knot formed and released in his belly.

He watched Naomi move like a heavenly body toward the front of the restaurant.

Was she dining alone? With friends? A man? He finished off his rum punch, hopped down off the three-legged stool and told the bartender to add the drink to his room tab. He left a tip and hurried toward the restaurant before he totally lost sight of her.

The spacious restaurant was set on the beach, enclosed on all sides with netting, with a thatched roof that had hurricane lamps hanging from its rafters. Circular tables covered in white linen dotted the planked floors in a horseshoe, leaving the center for dancing. The waiters all wore stiff white jackets and black slacks. The waitresses wore all black, with white aprons. Calypso music, mixed with a little R & B, played against the sound of the waves that rolled against the shore and the seagulls that cawed in the distance.

When he got to the restaurant's hostess and the check-in podium he saw that Naomi was being taken to her seat. He peered over heads and shoulders to see if anyone was joining her. The waitress gave her one menu. He smiled.

"How many tonight, sir?"

Brice blinked at the much-too-young-looking hostess. "Oh, uh, just one."

"Someone will seat you in a moment," she said with a musical lilt to her voice.

"Thank you." He stepped to the side and let the couple behind him move up while he kept an eye on Naomi.

"Right this way, sir," another young woman said, coming up to his side.

He followed her to the opposite side of the room from where Naomi sat. She handed him a menu and asked if she could get him a drink.

"Thanks. Yes. A rum punch."

"Right away."

Brice settled back against the rattan chair and

surreptitiously studied Naomi from behind the protection of his menu.

A waiter approached Naomi's table and placed a pitcher of water in front of her. He filled her glass while he spoke. When Brice saw her soft smile and the way her lips moved in thanks, heard the sound of her laughter at something that was said to her, he instantly knew that he'd been silly to have cast such a harsh judgment on her. It was his ego talking.

The waitress returned with his drink. "Are you ready to order, sir?"

He looked up at the round, pleasant face. He crooked his finger to draw her closer.

"See that young lady over there in the yellow?" He raised his chin in Naomi's direction.

"Yes, sir."

He went into his wallet, and took out a twenty-dollar bill. "That's for you." He stuck it in her apron pocket. "I need you to go over there and gently ask her if she would be interested in having a guest at her table for dinner."

The young lady smiled. "Of course." She walked across the room and approached Naomi. They talked briefly for a moment and then Naomi glanced around the room and her gaze landed on Brice.

Her eyes widened in surprise and excitement. She smiled and he could see her nodding her head. He was halfway across the room before the waitress could reach him.

He stood above her, feeling like a pimple-faced

teen at his first high school dance. "Can we start again?"

His voice moved through her like a wave of heat. She inhaled deeply to try to still the rapid beating of her heart.

"I'd like that," she said softly.

He pulled out a chair and sat down. "Brice Lawrence."

"Naomi Clarke."

The waitress returned and took Brice's and Naomi's dinner order. They both selected seared salmon and began with the house salad.

"So, you already told me that you were here on vacation."

She lowered her eyes in embarrassment and tugged on her bottom lip with her teeth. "Sometimes I can sound a little curt. It's not my intention."

He waved off her apology. "Forget it. I was being oversensitive. Must be too much sun." He chuckled and was rewarded with her smile. "How long will you be staying?"

"Two weeks. What about you?"

"That works out perfectly. So am I, or close to it. But I plan on enjoying my entire summer. After I leave here I'm off to Cancún, then I'm meeting friends in San Francisco."

Naomi thought about Alexis's counsel, what she'd said about just throwing caution to the wind and relaxing. She was on vacation. She would never have to see him again if things didn't work out.

The waitress approached and asked if she could refill any drinks. Naomi asked what Brice was drinking.

"I'll have one of those," she said. Her heart hammered in her chest.

"One rum punch coming right up."

"Where are you from?" Naomi asked, trying to get herself together.

"I live in New York. What about you?"

"Uh, Florida." *Where did that come from?*

"Really?"

Did he know she was lying? "Yes. Is that strange?"

"No," he shrugged it off. "I just don't think Florida when I see a beautiful woman like yourself. And no, that's not a line. I just think *retirement* capital when Florida comes to mind." He leaned a bit forward. "Obviously I have to readjust my thinking."

Her cheeks heated with pleasure. Being a woman of many, many words, she was at a total loss.

The music changed from calypso to something soft and slow. Several couples moved onto the dance floor.

"Would you like to dance?"

"Oh…I…couldn't…."

"Sure you could." He stood up and took her hand and gently pulled her to her feet. He rested his palm at that low dip in her back and led her onto the floor. When he found a good spot he turned her into his arms, and she nearly gasped when the full length of her body pressed up against his. For a moment her head grew light and the room seemed to shift, until he steadied her in his embrace. She felt as if she'd lost total control of her limbs. They wouldn't move.

"Relax," he whispered, holding her tenderly, not too close but close enough for him to feel her warmth, the beat of her heart and the slight tremors that ran up and down her body and tingled his fingertips.

He smelled so incredibly good, Naomi thought, and felt herself drifting easily into his embrace, miraculously following his lead without stepping on his feet.

"So, Ms. Naomi," he said, breathing into her hair. "How about if, in the time we have left on the island, we get to know each other?"

She titled her head back and looked up into his eyes. "I'd like that very much."

After all, she was a woman from Florida and after this island jaunt she'd never see him again.

Chapter 3

He was so easy to be with, Naomi realized as they ate and talked and laughed. He was funny, handsome, sexy and intelligent. She was surprised to learn that he was a high school math teacher after leaving a six-figure job in corporate America and had aspirations of opening his own school for young men.

"That's a monumental task," Naomi said. "But so desperately needed."

Brice nodded. "Our young black men are under siege. They need so much, and the system is set up to have them fail. When I was working on Wall Street, I was one of barely a half dozen men of color in my giant corporate building, and those other guys were working in the mail room or were on the cleaning crews. I'd go into meetings and be "the only one." And it's like that all over corporate America. Young black men are not in decision-making positions or making the money." He shook his head. "They need to be prepared and not prepared to work for someone else but to be entrepreneurs, inventors, thinkers. But that won't happen in educational institutions that don't have young black boys interests at heart. I can't change the world, but maybe I can start with one young man, one school at a time."

His voice and the fierce look in his dark eyes radiate the passion that he felt and the mission he believed himself to be on. You couldn't listen to him and not get swept up in his dream for a better future for young black men. "How far away are you from opening your school?"

His smile was only halfway there. "Not as near as I need to be. It will take some time, but I'm focused. I've been working on putting several things into place over the past year and a half. I'm getting closer." He turned his glass around in a slow circle on the table. "Funny, I haven't told anyone besides my best friend, Carl, about 'my school.'" He looked into her eyes.

Her heart pounded. "Oh. I'm…honored that you… told me."

"You're easy to talk to."

Was it the way he was looking at her or the rum punch that was making her head spin?

"I've been so busy talking about me, what about you? What do you do in sunny Florida?"

She swallowed through her suddenly dry throat. She'd already started this off on a lie. How could she say something different now? This was crazy. She should have never listened to Alexis. "I work at a bookstore and take classes at night," she blurted out, surprising herself with the ease of the flow. *Must come from years of reading fiction,* she thought in the back of her head.

"You keep surprising me," he said. "Which bookstore?"

"Uh, Greenlight Books. It's one of the small independent stores."

"And you said you were going to school. What courses are you taking?"

"African-American studies." At least that was something she could talk about with some confidence.

"That was my major in college."

"Really?" She leaned forward, ready to immerse herself in her favorite subject.

Before they realized it, several hours, along with a couple of drinks, had passed, the crowd had thinned and the waiter was bringing the bill.

Brice looked around. "Wow, where'd everybody go?" he joked.

Naomi became instantly flustered. She reached for her purse and knocked it onto the floor. They both reached for it at the same time and bumped heads. Jerking back and holding their foreheads, they looked at each other and burst out laughing.

Brice handed Naomi her purse. "Sorry about that," he chuckled. "Are you okay?"

"I'm perfectly fine. Nothing that a little brain surgery won't cure."

"Ahhh, the lady has jokes." He stood and extended his hand to her. "How about we walk off this food and those drinks."

"Sure." She took his hand, and when his long, strong fingers wrapped around hers something warm, then hot, then electrifying scurried up her arm and shot through her body.

"You okay?"

Brice was peering down into her face, his brow wrinkled with concern.

Naomi blinked and took a breath. "Yes. I'm fine."

"Oh, I thought I heard you moan. I want to be ready if I need to sweep you off your feet and carry you to your room." He grinned devilishly and pretended to flex his muscles.

For a moment she saw herself nestled in his arms, her head pressed into the curve of his neck, inhaling that alluring scent of his as he strode across the beach, up to her room, where he would kick down the door and the music would play and it would all go black.

She'd obviously lost her mind. *No more rum punch.*

She gave her head a little shake. "I don't think that will be necessary," she said, forcing her head to clear. "Ready?"

"After you."

Naomi led the way out, with Brice no less than a step behind her. His gaze trailed up and down her body, envisioning the curves, appreciating the understated but mesmerizing sway of her hips and the way the silk of her hair fell in soft wisps around the back of her neck, tempting him to touch them, run them through his fingers. It was a good thing he wasn't going to be in Antigua for long. He could easily see himself wanting to get seriously involved with a woman like Naomi Clarke. But they lived worlds apart, and if things worked out for him the way he hoped and planned, he wouldn't have the time needed to devote to a relationship. He took in her profile, set against the purple night sky, sprinkled with the white light of the stars and quarter moon, and he wished that things could be different.

They strolled along the beach, away from the hotel, and walked closer to the water. Naomi took off her shoes and felt oddly liberated and daring as she let the water and sand wash over her feet and seep between her toes. She giggled at the sensation, and Brice became intrigued by her joy at something so simple. Most of the women he knew would look at the experience as an annoyance, something to mess up their pedicure. A halo of a smile curved his mouth.

"How is it teaching high school kids?" Naomi asked, turning to look at him with a wide-eyed expression.

"It has its moments." He chuckled lightly. "It's not

so much the subject matter, it's more about seeing that bulb go off over their heads when they 'get it.' I teach in a really tough neighborhood in Harlem. Most of those kids are from broken homes, belong to gangs, have all kinds of havoc going on at home. A couple of my female students already have children. For most of them, their lives are on probation before they even get a chance."

Naomi heard the pain and the passion in his voice. He really cared. He wasn't just saying words to impress her. She knew exactly what he meant about that light bulb going off. And she so wanted to share with him her own experiences, give him some encouragement, but it was too late now. She'd already set off on a path of no return.

Instinctively, she took his hand and squeezed it. He turned to look at her. A hot jolt of electric current shot between them, shocking them both.

Brice stopped walking. His eyes grazed her face in a tender caress. Naomi felt a pulse begin to beat between her thighs. Her heart felt as if it was tumbling around in her chest as she watched his face come closer to hers, until his image blurred and his warm lips brushed against hers.

She couldn't breathe. She couldn't think. The instant was so perfect as to be surreal.

Brice pressed a tiny bit closer. The overwhelming craving to taste the full sweetness of her mouth had his arm snaking around her waist, pulling her closer. That only made this sudden, driving desire more urgent when he felt her body glide against his and his erection bloom hard and full.

He groaned deep in his throat as her lips parted ever so slightly and she allowed him to run the very tip of his tongue over the inside of their wet softness.

Brice held her and drowned himself in the lushness of her, let her essence seep through his skin and awaken sensations inside him that he'd put on the back burner. Now, with Naomi, all the jets were on full blast. What he wouldn't give to spend real time with her. Get to know her and get to make love to her the way he was imagining.

This was so unlike him. Women were a dime a dozen in New York. He could have his hands full if he wanted. The women he knew and had run across didn't rock his world, make him lose perspective and think about all the things he wanted to do to them. But this woman…this Naomi Clarke was not like all the others. It was as if she had woven some kind of spell over him from the moment he set eyes on her. She stirred up a burning thirst in him, and he wasn't going to ever be satisfied until his thirst was quenched.

Naomi felt weak all over, and her body was on fire. From deep inside she trembled. This wasn't her. This isn't what she did with a virtual stranger. But she couldn't help herself. She couldn't stop and she didn't want to. His mouth was like an irresistible gem that had to be captured and held. When his fingers pressed into her back and brought her closer, her own sighs floated into the night sky when she felt the bulge of his sex press against her.

It had been so long since she'd felt desire, and, more importantly, *desired* by a man. It emboldened her. And the fictitious life that she'd created was her shield. She could hide behind it. She could *be* a bookseller from the panhandle of Florida, who took classes at night and who was on a vacation in Antigua.

It didn't matter. This was a fantasy being played out in real life. For once, she was going to take a risk. She was going to give in to her feelings and not try to make sense of them.

If she would only have one night with Brice Lawrence, she was going to take it.

With great reluctance and pure willpower, Brice eased away from the simple kiss that had shaken him to the depths of his soul. He knew that if he didn't stop this spontaneous act, they would go much further than either of them were prepared for.

Naomi felt like Christmas morning. Brice's arms were the red ribbons that laced around her, holding her like a prized possession. She was lost in his arms, transported to a place of pure sensual pleasure with his kisses. She'd tossed aside her inhibitions, her no-nos, and simply went with the moment. When he pulled away, she'd instantly had a moment of doubt, of panic. What had she done wrong? But that wasn't it, she quickly realized. She understood when she looked up into his eyes that he had been in that same special place, and his words confirmed it.

He held her face in his palms and looked into the soft sparkle of her eyes, the questions that were reflected in them. "I…really didn't mean for that to happen," he said. "Yes, I did," he confessed. "But I don't want you to think that I'm just another guy on the make." He tried to collect his thoughts so that what stumbled out of his mouth made sense. "I can't explain it. There's something about you that…damn, I don't know." He shook his head in confusion and chuckled in spite of himself.

Naomi brushed his chin with her thumb. "You don't have to explain. For some things there are no words," she said, surprising herself. She'd always been one who lived by rationale. Everything had a reason and an explanation. But on this beautiful tropical island with this handsome, desirable, sexy man, under the moon and the stars…there were no words.

"Then I'm not losing it," he said.

"If you are, then so am I."

Brice drew in a long breath of relief and pulled her tight against him. He kissed the top of her head. "I probably should get you back to your room before I do something really crazy and strip you out of that sexy outfit right here on the beach." He took her hand and they walked back toward the hotel.

Naomi's heart pounded and her spirit smiled.

Chapter 4

Naomi felt like a small earthquake was going off inside of her by the time they reached the front door to her room. What happens next? Should she ask him in? Would that be too aggressive? *A little late to be thinking of being aggressive.* Her mind ran in circles.

"So..." he said on a long breath. He stood in front of her with her back to the door. "See you in the morning?"

"Sure. Yes."

"How about breakfast down on the beach?"

She smiled. "Sounds great."

"And what if I knock on your door at say, seven?"

"I'll be ready."

He stepped an inch closer. "And what if I knocked on your door...before then?"

Oh God, what was he saying? "Umm..."

He lifted her chin and smiled. "Don't worry. I won't put you on the spot. But I do want to make it clear that if I had my way, I'd be on the other side of your door making love to you."

Her insides jumped up the Richter scale. She couldn't breathe. She tried to speak, but no words came out. He leaned down and kissed her lightly on the lips. "See you in the morning."

"O-kay."

He turned and walked down the hall to the elevator.

Naomi's knees wobbled so badly she could barely stand up. It took her several tries before she could get her key card to slide through the slot and open the door.

Once on the other side of safety, she all but collapsed onto the first available club chair. Her pulse raced, her chest was damp and her clit was throbbing like a tiny heartbeat.

"Oh, lawd. What have I gotten myself into?" She took several deep breaths, then checked her watch. It was nearly two a.m. Alexis might still be up. She dug in her purse for her cell phone and tapped in Alexis's number.

She listened to the phone ring on the other end until Alexis's voice mail came on. Naomi babbled out a message and disconnected the phone. She pushed up from the chair, went to the bathroom and began getting undressed.

The evening with Brice played over and over in her mind while she stood under the pulse of the shower, as she ran the soapy loofah over her body. The water washed away the suds but not the heat that sat in her center and spread down the inside of her thighs. She relived his smile, his laughter, his scent, the feel of his hands around her waist, his lips on hers. She closed her eyes and allowed the sensations to take over and flow through her veins.

She imagined that the pulsing water was Brice's fingertips playing a concerto along the surface of her skin. Her eyelids fluttered. A soft moan slipped through her lips.

In the distance she heard knocking. She blinked, turned off the water and listened. There it was again. Her heart thumped. Brice? Did he really come back? She grabbed the thick robe from the hook on the door slipped it on and tugged the belt. She darted for the door then stopped a split second before pulling it open. She took a calming breath. "Yes?"

"Room service, ma'am," came the clearly Bahamian accent.

Whatever wild imaginings she may have had about Brice being on the other side of her door sputtered away like a pin-pricked balloon. She opened the door. Her eyes widened.

"Where would you like these, ma'am?"

The young man carried in a vase filled with blooming, brilliant tropical flowers.

"Uh, you can put them on the table by the balcony."

She stood at the open doorway thrilled down to her toes, and she couldn't wait for the young man to leave so that she could squeal in delight.

Moments later he was walking toward the door. He bobbed his head and waited. Naomi's brow arched in question. "Oh." Realization struck. She hurried across the room and dug through her wallet for a tip. He left with a big, bright smile. *Probably gave him too much*, she thought as she shut the door and darted to the other side of the room.

She gently parted the aromatic folds of the leaves and found a card pinned to a slender green stem.

"Just in case I messed up in any way tonight, accept this as my apology. If not then just enjoy them! See you at seven."

Naomi drew the embossed card to her chest and smiled. Then leaning forward, she inhaled the heady scent of the arrangement.

She could easily see herself with someone like Brice. If she had to write up a list of what she wanted in a man, everything about Brice would be on it. But none of that mattered. Their time together was limited and she had lied. Not to mention that they lived thousands of miles apart.

She took off her robe, tossed it on the side chair and slid naked under the cool white sheets. She turned on her side and gazed out upon the dark horizon that stretched into forever, and decided that it was too late to turn back now. She was determined to make their time together as bright and memorable as possible. It had been a while since she'd allowed herself to succumb to the charms of a man, let a man fill all those empty spaces inside of her. She hugged herself beneath the covers. What she was planning to do was deliciously dangerous.

It went against every iota of her being, and that's what made it so tempting. For the next two weeks Dr. Naomi Clarke was going to be tucked away between the pages of a book. And Naomi Clarke, woman on vacation, was going to take her place.

Naomi read the words on the card until she committed them to memory. With reluctance she turned off the bedside lamp and wished away the hours.

Brice arrived at the hotel's beachfront restaurant by 6:30 a.m. to make sure that the breakfast order that he'd placed before he went to sleep the prior evening was prepared and their table secure.

When he'd been on the phone with the hotel, ordering the flowers and arranging for breakfast, in the back of his mind he kept asking himself *what are you doing? Better yet, why?* He barely knew this woman, and yet he did. All the wooing and wining and dining wasn't his usual M.O., especially with someone he'd probably never see again. Although the Internet, Skype and cell phones kept the world well connected, he wasn't one for long-distance relationships. Maybe that was it, he concluded, while he was being shown to his table. The fact that it was temporary released him, and apparently Naomi, from any inhibitions.

But deep inside he knew that was only part of it. It was Naomi. Plain and simple. He couldn't explain it, but she'd totally thrown him off balance. Never before had he allowed himself to be seduced by no more than a beautiful smile. He'd seen plenty. Great body...but he'd had his share. It was something intangible. That spark that Carl always talked about feeling when he met his wife, Theresa. *Wife!* He chuckled to himself. He was definitely trotting down the wrong path.

He drew in long breath of salt-drenched air, leaned back in his seat and gazed out into the horizon. The rising sun splashed orange and gold across the crystal blue waters. He would make the most of every minute that remained.

"Good morning."

Her voice, low and rippling like the morning tide, raised the fine hairs on his arms. *Get it together, brother,* he cautioned himself before he dared to look at her fully. He raised his eyes and, like a dream come true, she stood in front of him. The honey color of her sundress matched the smooth tones of her skin, almost giving the illusion that she was naked. But of course that was simply his heated imagination.

He stood, and her smile competed with the sun.

Without thought, he leaned toward her and kissed her softly on the lips. The sensation of her moist mouth and soft lips, combined with the slightest whiff of her scent, was like a jolt of java. It shot to his head and spread through his veins. He eased back until her image came into focus. "'Morning."

Naomi's stomach was in the middle of a backflip. "Hi," she said on a breath that floated to him like a caress. "You weren't waiting long, were you?"

"No, not at all." He came closer and pulled out her chair. The weight of her breast grazed his arm as she sat down.

Naomi's breath rushed out in a soft gasp of pleasure at the contact. Her nipples hardened with anticipation.

"Sleep well?" he asked, settling down in his seat.

"Yes, I did. Once I got the thermostat adjusted, I slept straight through." She wouldn't tell him that her dreams were filled with him—dreams so potent that when she awoke she fully expected him to be right there next to her in the queen-size bed. She ran her tongue across her lips. "What about you?"

Brice watched her lips move, but even for a winning lottery ticket he couldn't tell anyone what she'd just said.

"Are you okay?"

He reached for his glass of water. "Yeah." He chuckled lightly. "Sorry, I was…thinking about what we could do today."

"Oh." She smiled brightly, then reached across the table and touched his hand. "Thank you for the beautiful flowers. They are absolutely gorgeous."

His eyes crinkled in the corners. "So, did you accept them for pure enjoyment, or restitution?"

She looked directly into his eyes. "Enjoyment."

"That's what I was hoping you would say."

She propped her chin on her palm. "Why did you think you may owe me an apology?"

His eyes moved slowly over her face. "For maybe coming on a little too strong."

"Do you honestly think that you did?" she gently probed.

"I'm going to be real honest with you. When I'm with you, for whatever reason, my good sense seems to escape me." He gave a self-deprecating laugh and slowly shook his head. "And that's all the confession I intend to make," he added, shifting the serious tone to a lighter one.

Naomi lowered her gaze, unable to withstand the intensity of his eyes. She fumbled with her fork, just as the waitress approached their table with two bowls of fresh fruit, much to her relief.

"Coffee or tea?" the waitress asked.

"Tea," they said in unison, then looked at each other and laughed.

"Coming right up."

"If nothing else, we have tea in common," Naomi said.

"Do you really think that's all we have in

common?" he asked, his words taking on a probing, teasing tone.

"Time will tell."

He lifted his glass and tipped it partially in her direction. "Touché'

"You were saying that you'd been thinking of what we could do today."

"I thought you might like to go into town and look around at some of the shops. We could have lunch there, and then I thought we could take the tour up into the mountains and see some of the mansions. The nightlife is pretty great, parties all over. I mean...I may be jumping ahead of myself. I'm sure you came here with some plans of your own, so—"

"No." She held up her hand. "Sounds wonderful. I really didn't have a clue about what to do with myself for a whole two weeks. I looked at a few of the brochures, but..." She shrugged her right shoulder.

"I totally understand. So we'll squeeze in everything that we can."

And then it would be over, she thought. But she wouldn't worry about that now. She'd have plenty of time for that.

The waitress returned with their tea and brought a platter of codfish cakes and callaloo. The spicy aroma was mouthwatering, and before they realized it, they'd tossed aside all propriety and dug in.

"Oh, my goodness," Naomi muttered, finishing off her third fish cake. "These are incredible."

"Hmm," Brice murmured with his mouth full. "It's my favorite."

"Now it's mine, too."

The restaurant began to slowly fill up with hotel guests, just as Brice and Naomi finished up their meal.

"I'm going to go to my room and get a few things," Naomi said. "What time did you want to leave?"

"I have some calls to make." He checked his watch. "How about we meet in the lobby about ten?"

"See you then." She started to move away.

Brice caught her wrist. She stopped and turned, her eyes widened in question.

He kissed her. "See you soon."

Her heart tumbled around in her chest. "Can't wait."

He let her go and she walked off, keenly aware of his eyes on her until she turned the corner toward her the side of the elevator banks. It was only then that she dared to breathe. She pressed the button and tugged on her lip with her teeth, removing the last of her lip gloss.

A trill of excitement, like a high note on a sax, rippled through her as the elevator ascended. She got off on her floor and walked down the corridor to her room.

She slid the key card through the slot and pushed the door open, just as her cell phone buzzed in her purse. While stepping inside, she pulled out her phone and saw that the call was from Alexis. She pressed Talk.

"Hey, Lexi."

"Hi, I got your message. You called pretty late. Is everything all right? You were rambling."

"I know, I know." She walked fully into the room and kicked off her sandals, then plopped down on the club chair. She put her feet up on the matching ottoman. "Where do I begin? I guess I should tell you that I took your advice."

"What! Now that's what I'm talking about. And it worked, didn't it?"

Naomi blew out a breath that preceded her smile. "Better than I could have imagined."

"Let me hear it, and don't leave anything out."

Naomi brought Alexis up to date, including her afternoon and evening plans with Brice.

"Whoa. I don't know what to say, Naomi. Other than you are a damned good student. I knew all those smarts you had would come in handy outside of a classroom."

They laughed.

"But I do hate lying. He seems like the kind of man I would want to be with. But now…"

"Listen, this is all about now. Not tomorrow or the day after. Enjoy yourself. Get loose. Get some old-fashioned loving with a fine, intelligent man. Then you pack your bags at the end of next week and come back to the real world."

Naomi sighed. "Yeah, you're right. I may as well enjoy it while I can."

"And girl, I know I don't have to tell you to use your own protection. I mean of course, if it gets that far."

Naomi flushed. She could barely imagine what it might be like to make love with Brice Lawrence. Her heart started racing just thinking about it. "I will, but I doubt it will go that far."

"Why? You said he told you that if he had his way he would be curling your toes. Well, not in those exact words, but you know what I mean. Sounds like he's hot for you." She paused. "Look, men do it all the time. Remember Stella in Terry McMillan's *How Stella Got Her Groove Back*?

"No."

Alexis shook her head. "Anyway, you need to get your groove back. I mean, come on Nay, there hasn't been anyone of note in your life since Trevor, and that was almost two years ago. If you don't use it, it might just dry up."

"Oh, stop," she chided, mildly embarrassed. She hadn't thought about Trevor in a long time, and that took some doing. They'd been seeing each other for nearly a year. She'd thought that he was the one. He was a professor at Morehouse, intelligent, fun, sexy— but a liar. He'd lied to her for the entire time they were together. All along he'd been seeing someone else, and she didn't find out until she got a call from his fiancée! That nearly broke her. She'd never been so hurt and humiliated in her life.

After that she buried herself in her books and work. Attaining the position of dean became her single focus. It filled her hours and her mind, but it didn't fill the empty space in her heart.

Alexis was right. She hadn't had sex in twenty-two months and counting. And up until she met Brice, she'd been able to convince herself that the celibate life was fine with her. But she knew better. As much as she might protest, she loved sex. She loved being sexual. She loved what a skilled man could do to her body and she to his. But she covered that all up under the guise of propriety, drab suits, minimal makeup, black pumps and a stereotypical teacher's bun. But there was another Naomi Clarke that was begging to come out.

"You still there?"

"Huh. Oh, sorry. What were you saying?"

"I was saying to just relax and enjoy yourself. And bottom line, Nay, no matter what I say, do what's in your heart to do."

Naomi thought about that while she changed clothes and prepared for her day and night ahead. She put her lipstick, her phone, room key, money and identification in her purse. Then she went to the dresser and took out her little makeup bag from the drawer. She unzipped it and stared at the pack of lubricated condoms. Before she could change her mind, she opened the box and took out two and tucked them in the zippered compartment in her purse.

Just in case, she thought as she headed out.

Chapter 5

Brice was looking forward to his day with Naomi with unexpected excitement. It felt more important than it should. He'd spent more afternoons than he could count with wonderful women. There was no real reason why he should feel so new, so scrubbed clean, as if he'd taken a hundred rain forest showers. But he did, and it was jolting—as if he'd walked in on a surprise party and was actually surprised.

His smiling reflection stared back at him. He felt genuinely good inside. He pulled his cotton polo shirt over his head and tucked it down into his slacks. A new kind of anticipation made him move with precision and purpose, from the clothes that he chose to wear to the cologne he splashed on his jaw to the extra care that he took with trimming the edges of his hair.

Every move and decision that he made was inexplicably with Naomi in mind. He wanted to please her, to see her smile and have her eyes take on the light, the way they did when something made her happy. For the life of him, he couldn't understand it. He felt as if he knew her, really knew her, even though that was impossible. And it was more than simple sexual attraction.

A part of him wished that's all that it was. At least that was something that made sense and was something that you could deal with and move on from. But there was this invisible string that kept tugging him in Naomi's direction, even though he knew the chances of it going any farther than these next days was slim.

He took his wallet from the top of the dresser and slid it into the back pocket of his slacks. If he didn't know better, he'd swear the woman put some mojo on him when he wasn't looking. He chuckled at the ridiculousness of that thought and headed out to meet her. His grandmother had been a great believer in signs and symbols and old African legends and sayings. For every event in one's life, his grandmother had a saying, a proverb or an herbal remedy to go with it. He chuckled to himself as he strode down the hallway to the elevator. He wondered what Grandma Mae would have to say to her grandson now.

When he arrived at the lobby he took a slow look

around to see if Naomi had already arrived. When his sweeping gaze found her, a burst of heat popped in the center of his chest. She was seated in the center of the room in the circular lounge area that had a waterfall as its centerpiece. From where he stood, she looked like a young girl instead of the very mature woman he knew her to be. Her long hair was pulled back and away from her face into a ponytail. She wore hoop earrings, a white tank top and white shorts that came halfway down her gorgeous thighs. Her legs were crossed and she was casually swinging one while she flipped through a magazine.

"Hey there."

Naomi glanced up and a smile lifted the corners of her glossy mouth, and he realized how much he liked that way her eyes tilted upward when she smiled.

"Hey." She put the magazine down on the table.

"Sorry to keep you waiting."

"Not a problem. I can very easily keep myself busy. Between catching a glimpse of some of these outfits…under the guise of reading a magazine I kept my time well occupied."

Brice chuckled at her mention of the outfits that some people had on. It was clear that some clothes were not made for *every* body.

"Ready?" He extended his hand and helped her to her feet.

"Lead the way."

He held her hand as they crossed the lobby, and nothing could have felt more natural to Naomi.

The pressure of his fingers around her hand was as comforting and familiar as her favorite quilt, making her want to snuggle up in it.

Last night, after dinner with him, she had a hard time believing that it had all actually happened—and to *her*. Especially after the fiasco at the poolside bar. There was that skeptical, analytical part of her that thought that he very well might not show up for dinner. That the night before had only been a nice diversion, a way not to spend the evening dining alone. *But then there was the kiss*, her inner voice whispered. Was that imagined? A put-on? And when she'd come down to breakfast he was there. It was some false hope, some wishful thinking on her part. She stole a quick glance at him just to check one more time that he was real.

"Since this is your first time, I thought you might be interested in the farmers' market. Great place to pick up some souvenirs for your family and friends back home."

"Perfect. Is it far?"

"About fifteen minutes. I rented a car."

"Really? Do you know how to drive on the wrong side of the road?"

He chuckled as he pushed the door open. They got hit with a blast of hot air that was in deep contrast to the almost arctic air of the hotel. "It took me a while to get the hang of it, but I won't run us into a ditch. How's that?"

She gave him a droll sideways glance. "That's comforting."

"We'll be fine. Promise."

They emerged onto the winding front entranceway of the Sandals Hotel. Immediately a red-jacketed valet was at their side.

"Yes, how can I help you? Do you need a taxi?"

"No actually, I rented a car."

"Oh, yes. Then please walk down to the booth and they will get your keys and your car, sir."

"Thank you." This time he put his arm around Naomi's waist. "This way, *madame*."

His arm felt too good, if that were possible. Not possessive, not matter-of-fact, as if he had the right, but simply there where his arm was supposed to be at that moment. The sensation of something greater than them bringing them together toyed with her head, even though she was a firm believer in fact not fate. She pulled in a short breath. *Let it go, Naomi,* she told herself. *Relax and enjoy. Don't analyze.*

They walked up to the booth and Brice gave his name. Moments later a navy blue Honda hybrid pulled up in front of them. The driver hopped out and came around to open the passenger door, handing the key to Brice, who gave him a tip before helping Naomi into the car. He came around front and got in behind the wheel.

"This will be a double new experience," Naomi said while she fastened her seat belt.

"What's that?" He adjusted the mirrors.

"One, driving on the wrong side of the road, and two, in a hybrid. I've never been in one before."

"Me neither," he said, looking for the ignition.

"What?" Her voice had risen two octaves.

He turned to her with bad-boy merriment in his eyes. "Just kidding." He stuck the key into the ignition, put the car in Drive and pulled off.

"Do you want the windows open, or do you prefer the air?"

"Let's keep the windows open," she said. "I want to get the full flavor of the island."

"You'll get a great breeze. I drive really fast."

Her head snapped in his direction, her eyes wide.

He reached over the gear/shift and patted her thigh. "Just kidding."

"Oh, I see it's going to be one of those days," she teased.

"It's going to be a spectacular day," he said, turning for an instant to look at her. And then he winked.

The view on the trip into town was completely amazing. The brochures focused on the beaches and restaurants and the mountain views. They didn't show pictures of rural Antigua, where the real people lived in communities that were taken out of the pages of history books. Unpaved roads; homes made of wood and stone; goats that roamed the streets as freely as the people; children playing barefoot; roadside vendors selling sweets and handmade crafts. Old, worn men and women sitting on drooping porches and steps. It was a completely different world, and she wasn't sure if she should feel enlightened or saddened by what she saw.

"I know what you must be thinking," Brice said, slipping into her thoughts.

"What am I thinking?" She angled her body in the seat to get a better look at him.

"All of this poverty surrounded by lush beauty." He glanced quickly at her.

She nodded her head. "It's like this in so many places," she said. "In parts of Mississippi, there are still plantation homes and sugarcane fields less than two streets away from the palatial government offices."

"The ninth ward in New Orleans," Brice added.

"Southside of Chicago. Huge parts of Detroit, New York." She shook her head. "It's a shame and a disgrace that we're allegedly one of the richest countries in the world, and yet we have people who live with virtually nothing."

"The haves and have-nots. That's why I need to get to our young boys while they are young. Get in there and show them the power of education and what it can bring you. It's the only way out."

"I completely agree."

They launched into a deep discussion about the educational system, testing practices and curriculum. Brice was amazed that Naomi was so versed in the details of educational institutions and had many solid ideas of her own on how things could be changed.

"I'm totally impressed," he said when she'd finished conveying her thoughts on revamping the testing system.

She blinked back her surprise. "Impressed?"

"Yes. If I didn't know better I'd think you were down there in the trenches of teaching." He grinned.

Her stomach jumped. She could kick herself. She was a bookseller that worked and lived in Florida. Not a tenured professor at an HBCU, or Historically Black College or University, in Atlanta. Her smile fluttered like birds' wings. "I, um, just try to keep up with the news." She swallowed and turned to face forward in her seat.

He looked at her for a moment, thrown off by the shift in her seat and in her tone. "I wish more people were like you, and paid attention to what was happening," he said, wondering if he'd hit an unseen button.

But he didn't have time to address it as they were entering St. John, the capital city of Antigua. It would take every bit of skill and dexterity to maneuver the tight, congested streets that overflowed with cars, people, vans and carts, on roads that were barely wide enough for a one-lane roadway, let alone two, with no real sidewalks to speak of.

The architecture, however, was breathtaking, with the church of St. John as the centerpiece. The cobblestone streets were lined with quaint businesses, fruit-and-vegetable stands and craftsmen, while the aroma of sautéed seafood and seasoned vegetables wafted in the air. The busy streets bustled with tourists and residents intent on selecting the best bargains and jockeying for position on the narrow avenues.

Miraculously, Brice found a parking spot which was actually half on the curb and half in the street—in a line with all of the rest of the parked cars. He got out and helped Naomi to her feet.

"Wow," Naomi breathed in awe when she got out and began to look around. The buildings, small and tightly packed together, all had a welcoming openness about them. Splashed in bright tropical colors, it was like walking through the feathers of a peacock.

Brice took Naomi's hand, and she held on tight as they bobbed and weaved between the people and the carts, the cars and the buildings.

She moved closer to him as they squeezed by a brightly dressed woman with a cart of fresh island fruit.

"Those look delicious," Naomi said, following the woman's cart with her eyes.

"Want to try something?"

"Sure."

They backpedaled a bit until they were in front of her. Naomi's eyes ran over the array of fruits.

"Try the tamarin," the woman suggested, holding up a wrapped piece of what looked like a ball of brown sugar that had been melted and then shaped. "It's sweet, chewy and a bit spicy." She held it up to Naomi and smiled a wide gap-toothed smile.

Naomi took the candy from the woman's hand. "I'll give it a try."

"Make that a half dozen," Brice said, "and how about some Kiwi fruit and a two mangos." Then he turned to Naomi. "Sorry, I don't share my mangos. So you'll have one of your own."

Naomi laughed.

"See anything else you like?" he asked her.

She wanted to tell him what she really thought, that for as long as it was possible, he was what she wanted, but of course she didn't. "This is fine."

"Great. How much?" he asked the woman.

She gave him a total and put his purchases in a bag. They continued down the street and spent the next few hours exploring the shops and the museum, where Naomi bought a piece of pottery for Alexis.

"How do you feel about water?" Brice asked.

"Water? What do you mean?"

"Can you swim?"

"Enough to save myself."

"Do you mind getting your pretty white outfit a little wet?"

"Depends," she said, angling her head to the side in question. "Just how wet are we talking?"

"Come on. We'll find out together." He took her hand and they headed off toward the docks, where an array of catamarans were moored.

Naomi's eyes widened.

"In for a bit of sailing on the Caribbean?"

Her smile was radiant. "I'll try anything once," she said, surprising herself.

"Great. I love a woman who has a sense of adventure." They walked together toward the rental stand.

Naomi moved away to look more closely at the beautiful boats, while Brice talked with the rental agents. Moments later he was at her side.

"There will be another ship sailing off in about a half hour. The tour is along the beaches and around the mountainsides. Food and refreshments are on board."

"Sounds wonderful."

He stepped up to her, taking her by surprise, and kissed her softly on the lips.

"I've been waiting to do that all day."

"What took you so long," she said in a heavy whisper, looking up into his dark eyes.

"Why don't I just make up for lost time?" He leaned down and kissed her again, not a brushing of warm lips, but a full, deep and stirring kiss, and it made her head light and her heart race.

He stepped back with his hands still around her waist, and looked at her with pure fascination, asking himself for the countless time what it was about Naomi Clarke that had gotten under his skin.

Chapter 6

They spent the afternoon sailing around the island, sipping juices, munching on island delicacies and absorbing each other's company. There were several other couples aboard, and when the captain turned on the music the sailing turned into an onboard party. By the time they returned to the hotel they had been thoroughly entertained, were wobbly on their feet and totally enamored of each other.

Naomi wasn't sure if it was the breathtaking atmosphere, the warm rays of the sun, the enchanting lifestyle of the Caribbean, or if it was simply being with Brice that had her feeling as if she was floating on air. She could not remember feeling so close, so compatible with a man. They touched on so many subjects, from politics to religion, and family, movies and music. They enjoyed and appreciated so much of the same things in life and were passionate about each of them. How she wished that she had not lied to him, that she had started this all off the right way. That was the only shadow hovering around her world of happiness.

There had been so many times throughout the day that she wanted to tell him the truth. But she had no way of knowing how he would react. She couldn't stand the idea of what he would think of her when she did. Best to just leave it alone, she continued to remind herself when the words were sliding up her throat and moving across her tongue. She didn't want anything to mar the magical time they were having together.

They returned to the hotel exhausted but happy, laughing and talking the entire way back about the sights they'd seen throughout the day.

"Tired of me yet?" Brice asked as they entered the lobby of the hotel.

She turned to look at him. "No. Why would you think that?"

"Good. Because I want to spend the rest of the evening with you. I made dinner reservations in the hotel restaurant, and then we can see what happens." His gaze held her in place. Her pulse throbbed in her ears.

"I'd like that very much," she managed to say.

"That's the answer I was hoping for."

They crossed the lobby hand in hand and walked toward the elevators.

"Too bad we're on different sides of the hotel," she said.

"And why is that, pretty lady?"

She turned to face him fully. "Makes it more difficult to tap on your door in the middle of the night."

His dark eyes explored her face. "Who says we have to wait until the middle of the night?" His voice lowered and stirred the cauldron of heat that had been simmering in her center all day.

The elevator doors whooshed open and several people got off, laughing and talking, oblivious to the currents of tension that popped like downed electrical wires between Naomi and Brice.

The door began to close. Naomi took his hand and pulled him inside just in time. He backed her up against the far wall, his hands skimming her curves while his lips played teasing games with her cheeks, her nose, her fluttering eyelids, the plumpness of her parted lips.

Naomi sighed into his mouth, her internal heat combusting with his, causing a groan to rise from deep inside Brice. He stroked her cheek, ached to free her hair so that he could thread his fingers through it.

The bell dinged. They eased apart just as the doors opened. Brice stood in the threshold of the door while

Naomi walked out. She glanced at him when he fell in step at her side, disbelieving what she was about to do. This wasn't some romance novel fantasy that she was reading. She was the heroine of her very own fairy tale and she was about to make love to her very own hero.

They reached her door and she fumbled in her purse for her key card. Finally she managed to get it out.

"Here, let me." Brice took the card and slid it down the slender opening. The door buzzed.

Naomi's heart hammered in her chest. What in the world was she doing? She nearly gasped when she heard the door shut behind them, and the enormity of what she was on the verge of doing closed in around them.

"Wait," he said. He placed his hands on her shoulders and looked searchingly into her eyes. "I know that we're both adults and this is a beautiful island and people can get easily swept up in the magic of it all." He paused a moment when she stared into the same questioning look that she knew reflected her own, she believed that for Brice this was not just some quick sex with an available woman. It meant something and he wanted to be as sure about her as she was about him. "I just want you to know that this is not some casual thing that I do."

She drew in a long breath. "Me, either," she whispered and stepped inside.

For a moment they both stood in the center of the room—waiting.

"Umm, make yourself comfortable," she said.

"Pretty nice place you have here," he teased, hoping to ease the knot of tension that was choking them both.

She sputtered a nervous laugh. "I'm sure we have the same designer." She drew in a breath. "Want something from the bar?"

"Sure, if the water is cold that would be great."

She walked over to the small bar and unlocked it for the first time since her arrival, and was surprised at the array of contents: soda, liquor, water, chocolates, snacks. She took out two bottles of water and handed one to Brice, who had strolled out onto the terrace.

"Thanks. This really is a beautiful place," Brice said, twisting the cap off of the bottle. He took a long, cool swallow. "I guess that's why I keep coming back." He turned to her and leaned against the railing. "Or maybe I kept coming back in the hopes of finding something…or someone."

Naomi swallowed. "Did you?"

"I'd like to think so, Naomi. I know we live hundreds of miles apart, but maybe we can work something out. Actually, if things go as planned I may not be that far away from you after all."

"What do you mean?"

"I don't want to jinx it. I'll know for sure in a few weeks. I'll tell you about it then. But no matter what happens, I want to see you again." He grinned. "In the real world—and see how it goes."

"Are you sure about that?"

"As sure as I can be at the moment. And that's being perfectly honest."

Honest, a word that had been missing from her vocabulary since they'd met. The thought of finding a way to work out the distance between them was more than she could have hoped for. But the reality was that he wouldn't be visiting her in Florida.

"Brice, I…"

"Sssh." He pressed a finger to her lips. "Let's just see what happens, okay? No promises. The last thing I want to do is disappoint you if things don't work out."

Her gaze danced over his face. She was so torn. What should she do? Tell him before it went further? Keep lying to him? She should have never listened to Alexis!

But all rhyme and reason was swept from her thoughts when he stole her breath with a searing kiss. She felt herself melting into the strength of his arms, transported on the bed of his lips, tantalized by the sweetness of his tongue that teased hers.

Her arms slid around his neck, his around her waist, pulling her closer so that there was no space, no air between them. His lips drifted down to the pulse in her throat and she trembled with delight. He nuzzled her there, nibbled, drifted lower to the V-opening in her top, to savor the swell of her breasts.

Currents of energy ran in waves up and down the insides of her thighs, weakening her knees. If he was not holding her so securely, she was certain that she would drift to the floor like an unfastened skirt.

His hands moved slowly up and down her back. His thumbs grazed the underside of her breasts and she moaned in pleasure. He pressed closer to her and she felt the strength of his desire throb between her trembling thighs.

She felt light-headed and full of her own feminine power all at the same time, knowing that it was she who sparked Brice's longing. She wanted him. She wanted to know what he felt like beneath her fingers, inside of her.

She drew in a breath and eased back from his hold. She took his hands in hers and led him back into her bedroom. She pulled the drapes across the windows of the terrace, submerging the room into an intimate dimness.

Naomi boldly pulled her top over her head and tossed it to the floor, and even in the soft light she could see the burning in his eyes as he looked at her. Her chest rose and fell as she watched him draw closer. He reached behind her and loosened the clip that held her hair, and watched in admiration as it fell softly to her shoulders. Her ran his fingers through it, clasping the back of her head as he drew her to him.

A ragged groan tumbled across his lips as his mouth hungrily met hers. His fingers released her hair and trailed down her back. The snap of her bra opened and he slid the straps down her shoulders, then pulled it away from her body, tossing the white lace to the floor.

For a moment he was transfixed by her beauty: she was perfect, like something right out of his imagination. Reverently, he touched her as if she were more delicate and precious than fine china.

Naomi sucked in air through her teeth as the tender pads of his fingers stroked the rise of her breasts and grazed languidly back and forth over the dark nipples, awakening them into hard, needy buds. He lowered his head and brought one of the tender fruits to his mouth.

"Ohhh." Naomi's head dropped back, her body instinctively arched and her eyes squeezed shut as he gently suckled one, then the other, then back again, until she thought she would go mad with desire.

Brice carefully eased her back toward the bed. Naomi felt the back of her knees make contact with the mattress. She tugged Brice down and they tumbled together onto the downy-topped mattress.

Naomi giggled in delight and wrapped her arms and legs around him. Brice pulled her flush against him before he dipped his head between the sweet mounds of her breasts. His hands caressed the tautness of her stomach, the dip of her waist, while his mouth seared her skin wherever it touched. She writhed with pleasure, her soft moans stirring Brice beyond his wildest imagination.

His growing need for her pushed and pulsed against the confines of his slacks. Naomi reached down between their tightly knitted bodies and stroked the hard rise. Brice gritted his teeth, groaned with pleasure. It took total willpower not to rip the rest of her clothes from her body and bury himself between her silky thighs. But he knew he had to take his time, commit to memory every sigh, every move, every kiss—the feel of that first moment of intimate connection. More importantly he wanted Naomi to remember.

Naomi's slender fingers cupped him, massaged him until he could barely think clearly. As much as he thrilled to her touch, it would be his undoing. Reluctantly, he pulled her hand away and went to work getting her out of her shorts and her lace panties, until she was completely bare and lush before him. He took a moment to let his eyes and hands roll over her from the top of her head to the bottom of her feet. His only objective at the moment was to make love to every inch of her honey-colored skin.

"No, wait," Naomi managed to say, as if coming up from under water. She pushed her palms against Brice's chest and flipped over to get out from under him. She sat up on her knees.

Brice didn't know what he had done wrong. This couldn't be happening. "Na—"

"Sssh." She put her finger to his lips. A wicked

smile teased her mouth. "Why should I be the only one in the room with no clothes on?"

"Aw, woman, you had me there for a minute." He pulled his shirt over his head, unbuckled his belt and unzipped his slacks.

Naomi's stare was glued to his every move. Her nostrils flared as she watched him undress. He got off the bed and stepped out of his pants and then his shorts. Naomi drew in a short, sharp breath. He was perfection. Her clit jumped in response, and the welcoming wetness made her slick and ready. Their eyes locked onto each other. Brice came toward the bed. Naomi drew closer on her knees. Naomi stretched her arms toward him and he came willingly. The tips of her nails grazed across his chest then down across the hard-rippled stomach. She breathed deeply and took him into her palm. Brice's entire body stiffened as a wave of pleasure shot through him. Her hands were like warm butter as they slid up and down his length.

"Girl, girl, girl," he groaned. "Ahhh." He braced his palms against her shoulders and for a moment simply closed his eyes and let her do her thing. Until the pleasure began to overwhelm him. His breathing escalated. His erection was ready to burst. He clasped her wrist to stop her steady stroking.

She looked up at him, her eyes shining in the twilight. Her lips parted. Before she could react, Brice had her down on the bed, the weight of his body pinning her beneath him, her long legs spread on either side of him. He supported himself on his forearms before he began his slow and deliberate conquering of Naomi Clarke.

Brice kissed her deeply, the play of his tongue with hers an erotic dance as old as time. He longed to be everywhere at once, but he wanted to taste her sweet skin. He let his lips and his tongue create a sizzling path, taking stops at her neck along the lift of her breasts, down the fluttering dip of her stomach, to hover for an instant above the seat of her sex. He gently spread her thighs and brushed his face against the soft down of her hair. Naomi shuddered. His lips and tongue grazed and caressed the insides of her thighs as he held her. Then his tongue flicked across the hard bud that danced to the tune he played with it.

Naomi gripped handfuls of the sheets, crying out as her body arched in pleasure.

Like candy he licked and sucked and licked and stroked, while Naomi rocked her hips against the mastery of his mouth—quicker, faster, as the sensations roared up and down her limbs. Her head spun, heat rose from her damp flesh. Her cries had dissolved to whimpers, begging for release.

"Please," she whispered, her voice hoarse and jagged. "Please."

But for Brice it was the nectar of life, and hers was sweet and plentiful. He didn't want to stop. He thrilled at being able to bring her such pleasure. That's what making love was all about, bringing joy to someone else. And as much as he didn't want to stop, he knew that he should.

Slowly, he lifted his head and gently stroked her trembling thighs and stomach to soothe and settle her. Her chest heaved and shuddered as the waves continued to flush through her.

Brice eased his way up her body, capturing her legs over his arms and bringing them up to his chest as the hard tip of his penis pressed against the hot, wet opening and dipped down inside.

The instant was so explosive that they both erupted in a duel of sound. Shivers ran up Brice's spine as her warmth enveloped him and gently squeezed. He couldn't move, the sensation was too incredible to risk losing even for an instant; but instinct took over. The human need for satisfaction, for wanting more of something good, pushed him in and out and out and in. Deep and not so deep, slow but fast. Whatever it took to keep her calling his name, her fingers in his back, her legs locked around his hips, her breasts pressed to his chest, her lips melded with his. Whatever it took.

Tears of unimaginable pleasure hung from the corners of Naomi's eyes. The weight and length of Brice filled her in a way that she could not explain. It was not just her body that he'd entered, it was her soul. She opened not just her legs to him, but that space of who she was as a woman. And without a doubt, he put his stamp on it. His every move inside her, above her, along her, was beyond sweet. He'd taken her *there*. But what was more frightening, more tantalizing to realize, was that with each stroke, every rotation of his hips, every time he hit her spot with the head of his dick, she knew there was more to come. She could feel it ascend from the balls of her feet and slide up the inside of her legs, making her entire body quake. Then it moved upward to her belly, and spread like wildfire to her arms her fingertips. And all of that energy, all of that feel-good shot to her vagina and shook it like a rag doll, tossing her from this place on earth to somewhere beyond the stars. She felt Brice's strong arms slide beneath her to hold her as he pushed deeper while her climax intensified, the grip and release so powerful that it sucked the essence from Brice with such force that he felt electrified, his cry strangled in his throat, his body a live wire of feeling that splashed a stream of relief to cool their flames.

Naomi could hear her pulse still pounding in her temples as her racing heart began to slow and the tremors began to ease. She held on to the life raft of Brice's strong back to keep from going adrift. His embrace was secure and comforting, and a part of her knew this was who Brice Lawrence was. At the core of him, he was secure and comforting and oh, so loving.

He tenderly kissed the tiny pulse beat in her throat, and with much regret pulled out of her hold on him and rolled onto his back. He slid his arm beneath her and pulled her close. Naomi nestled against him and, lulled by the steady beat of his heart, drifted off into a deep, satisfied sleep.

Chapter 7

When Brice stirred, his first coherent thought was that what had happened between him and Naomi had to have been a dream. Nothing in this world could have been that magnificent. And when he opened his eyes and looked at the empty space next to him, he began to feel that maybe he did dream it all. But that would not account for the throb in his groin or the dampness of his body and the twisted sheets.

He drew in a breath and pushed himself up onto his elbow and tried to make out the shapes in the room. He looked toward the terrace, and reflecting the light of the moon was a body huddled in a chair.

He sat up fully, tossed his legs over the side of the bed and stood. He grabbed the sheet and gathered it around his waist, crossed the room and opened the terrace doors and stepped outside.

Naomi looked up, and Brice would have swore that her expression was almost angelic, as if she might not be real, but some exquisite apparition that he'd conjured. So he reached out and touched her hair to scatter any doubts. She clasped his hand and brought it to her cheek.

Brice swung down to sit beside her on the lounge chair.

"I thought I might have imagined it all," Brice said.

"So did I," she whispered. "I kept looking back at you in the bed to make sure it wasn't all in my head." She lowered her eyes then looked at him fully. "I never expected this. I don't want you to think that this is what I do. I—"

"Don't. Don't worry about explaining something that can't be explained. If anything, I think more of you now than before. You're an absolutely incredible woman."

They stared at each other for a few moments, savoring the memories that they'd created.

Naomi drew in a long, cleansing breath and took both of Brice's hands in hers. She leaned forward and looked him deeply in the eyes. "I'm starving," she said.

Brice tossed his head back and burst out laughing. He pulled her to her feet and draped his arm around her waist. "Me, too. Let's get some room service up in here."

After placing their order and being told that it would be at least a half hour, they decided to take a quick shower and be relatively presentable when room service arrived. Suddenly for Naomi, who had totally thrown caution to the wind, she was concerned about "how things might look." It was her old habits kicking in.

While she was reliving the moments with Brice, tangled and twisted and sweaty in her bed, she heard a knock on the bathroom door, followed by its opening. She peeked around the shower curtain and Brice poked his head in the door.

"Thought we could save some time," he hinted with a wink.

Naomi pouted, then dramatically drew back the curtain, revealing her slick, sudsy, sexy body. She crooked her finger, beckoning him to step beyond the curtain.

"You don't have to ask me twice," Brice said, covering the space in two long strides. He stepped into the shower and reached around Naomi for the soap and began lathering her breasts, then her stomach, down her legs and back up again. Then he turned her around and repeated the process. But when he was done he moved her to face the opposite wall with her back to him so that he could continue to caress and stroke her front.

Naomi's oversensitized body shot back into overdrive as Brice reached around her and down between her legs to play with her. She shuddered, moaned and was thankful for the railing in front of her that kept her from sliding down the tiled walls. Brice pushed up against her and the heft of his erection demanded entry. He ground his hips against her and she moved in unison with him until neither of them could stand the denial a moment longer.

Naomi grabbed the railing and bent from the waist, offering herself to him. Brice leaned forward and began planting tender kisses along her spine, while he continued to find new games to play between her legs. And when she least expected it, she gasped and gripped and shuddered as Brice rode up inside her.

"Ohhh, oh, my..ahhh." She sucked in air through her teeth and undulated her hips in time with Brice's rhythm.

He clamped her hips between his palms and reared back just enough to get that toe-curling angle, so he could move and watch them bump and grind against each other at the same time.

"Hmmm, baby," he groaned, feeling the jaw-dropping end coming near.

Naomi realized it, too. She felt the swelling inside her, the sudden insistence, the deeper, faster thrusts. She lifted herself on her toes and did a hard three-sixty with her hips. The move made Brice dig his fingertips into her hips as his strangled cry mixed with the rushing water—all in concert with the explosion that went off deep inside Naomi's belly and nearly brought her to her knees.

Brice held on to her until their tremors subsided, then he pulled out and helped her to stand up. He turned her around to face him, still stunned by what this woman had done to his body and his mind.

He pulled in a long breath and slowly shook his head.

"What?" she said, as the water continued to cascade over them.

"I wish I knew," he said.

She smiled, leaned up and kissed him softly on the lips. "If it helps any, I feel the same way."

He drew her to him and cocooned her in his arms. He was going to have to find a way to make this work. The hell with distance. Then truth insinuated itself in his thoughts. He had an agenda, a plan. And the plan did not include getting his head all messed up with a woman who he'd have to jump through hoops to see. A part of him was willing. But there was the other part that knew it was ridiculous. Hopefully, in the light of his real life, his time with Naomi would simply be an exquisite memory and he could move forward with his plans. Only time could tell.

The next week and a half seemed to fly by, but Naomi and Brice tried to spend every minute of it together. They played the roles of tourists to the hilt, going on every excursion and tour they could find. They shopped, they ate, they swam, sailed, fished and whenever the opportunity presented itself they had mind-blowing sex—up on the mountainside, below deck on the rented yacht, in a hidden cove on the beach, in a storage room they'd found open at the museum. It was wild, dangerous and decadent, and they both seemed to happily feed off the excitement.

Naomi had changed from the woman she was when she arrived, to this lusty, insatiable woman. So much as that there were moments when she would look in the mirror and be stunned by the dark and uninhibited look in her eyes. She felt free, and powerful and sexy and desirable, all the things she shoved to the back of the top shelf of her closet when she'd broken up with Trevor.

Brice had peeled back all of the layers of books and protocol, of heartache and distance, and uncovered a brand-new Naomi.

Trevor had been her first serious relationship, at least it had been serious to her. The sex between them was good, not that she'd had a lot of experience to compare it to, and certainly nothing that made her world turn upside down. Trevor coaxed her out of her shell. She thought she was happy. She thought she was complete. She thought she'd given the best of herself. But this thing with Brice was almost beyond what she had the words to explain. What was she going to do when it ended? What was she going to tell him when he asked to come see her or contact her? Even Alexis was at a loss for a workable suggestion.

All she kept mumbling was, "I didn't tell you to fall for him." A lot of good that sentiment was doing her now.

Today was their last day together. Brice had a noon flight to Cancún. They made frenzied, passionate, clinging love throughout the night and into daybreak, knowing instinctively that it would probably be the last time.

Over a breakfast of fruit and eggs and fresh squeezed mango juice, they were uncharacteristically quiet, not wanting to lie about possibilities, but not wanting to part without offering any.

When they did talk, it was about inconsequential things—the way the waves rolled to the shore, the tart taste of the kiwi, needing to get more suntan lotion. All the things to keep them from talking about the thing that needed to be said: what were they going to do after today?

And time, as it does when you need it the most, seemed to race by, and then they were standing in front of the reservation table while Brice had his bags loaded onto the van that would take him to the airport.

They stood together—and not. Looking at each other, but avoiding real eye contact in case they might see something that would make them say something that would change everything. So they didn't, because they couldn't change anything at all.

"We're ready, sir," the driver said, holding the door open for Brice.

"Sure. Thanks." He looked down into Naomi's eyes and saw his own hopes and uncertainties reflecting back at him. "Listen, I know it will be difficult, but let's see where this can go. You have my number. I'll be back in New York in about four weeks. But I promise I'll call you before then."

The burning in her eyes made his handsome image hazy and uneven around the edges, and the grip that sadness had on her allowed her to only nod her head in agreement. *Sure*, she thought, but didn't say that if there was any possibility of there being a chance she'd made that impossible.

Brice took her cheeks in his palms and tilted her face up to his. The warmth of his eyes, like the rays of the sun, was too bright for her to stare into, and she looked away an instant before the heat was cooled by the tears that slipped from the corner of her eyes. His lips kissed them away, and then she tasted the salt of her tears when his mouth covered hers.

And before she was ready, before she had a chance to confess the only thing that plagued the wonder of their affair, she found herself watching the van pull off—and she waved and cried and offered up a fluttering smile like a war bride watching her man go off to parts unknown.

She turned away. And when her gaze looked out beyond the horizon, across the water, she knew that her real life was a plane ride away, and that all *this* would soon become a memory as distant and unreachable as where the earth meets the heavens.

Chapter 8

Alexis was at the airport to meet Naomi, and one would think she was welcoming home a rock star. She came loaded with a bouquet of flowers and a Flip camcorder to record every moment.

Naomi walked into her welcoming arms, both of them laughing and hugging and asking and answering questions one on top of another. But it was like that with them, they were always feeding off of each other's energy. Alexis was Naomi's one true friend, the person she could be her real self with, quirks and all. And that's why Alexis knew that the smile and the bright eyes and the chatter was only a cover-up for what Naomi wasn't quite ready to talk about.

But she would, Alexis knew that. They were girl-friends. And that's what girlfriends did.

Their friendship dated back to college when they were both undergrads at Spelman and then they'd both gone off to New York and were roommates during their graduate studies at Columbia University. They roamed the streets of Manhattan together, burned the midnight oil, encouraged each other, permed each other's hair. It was Naomi who always cautioned the gregarious Alexis on her array of adoring men and it was Alexis who would slam Naomi's textbook closed and drag her out on Friday nights. It was Naomi who sat with Alexis in the planned parenthood clinic and cried with her over what she'd had to do. And it was Alexis who pushed Naomi back out into the world after Trevor's betrayal even when Naomi wanted to bury her head in the sand. They were girlfriends, sisters through and through. Night and day.

Alexis hooked her arm through Naomi's as they navigated their way to baggage claim, talked about the latest Bernice McFadden book that was getting so much well-deserved attention, the laundry that Alexis had allowed to pile up. "I just keep buying new clothes," she'd joked, and that made Naomi laugh. Clothes were Alexis's Achilles' heel. She'd been known to blow an entire paycheck on new outfits, rather than take the mounds of clothes that she had to the laundry and the cleaners. Naomi simply tossed it off as one of Alexis's quirks. She loved her anyway.

"How's mom?" Naomi asked, as they watched the luggage carousel go around for the third time without Naomi's bags on it.

"She is doing so much better. Got the home attendant in place. The doctors say she is a miracle woman. But it was scary, Nay. Thought I was going to lose her."

Naomi squeezed her close. "That old bird is too tough. She will outlive us all."

"I know that's right," Alexis said and sniffed. "Listen, I figured you'd be beat from the flight, and they never give you any real food on the plane, so I had lunch delivered to my house."

"Delivered?"

Alexis reared her neck back. "Girl, you know I don't cook, especially in the middle of the day."

Naomi shook her head and chuckled. "Fine with me. What are we having?"

"A little bit of everything!"

"Girl, you are too much." She lifted her head toward the slow-moving conveyor belt. "Here they come. I was getting worried."

"Hey, I have plenty of clothes to spare if yours didn't show up," Alexis teased, hoisting one of the bags off the belt while Naomi got the other.

"Thanks but no thanks. Where did you park?"

"I'm right in the lot on the other side."

They took off in that direction, pulling the bags behind them.

"You look good," Alexis said, once they were all buckled up and backing out of the parking spot.

"The Caribbean sun will do that to you. I wish you could have been there. Antigua is truly a paradise."

"I know, I know. One of these days I'm going to make that trip."

Naomi grew quiet, almost as if she had sunk inside herself, just leaving the image of a shadow behind.

Alexis glanced at her friend from the corner of her eye. "You okay?" she gently asked.

Naomi bobbed her head. "I will be. I have plenty to keep me busy. School opens in a few weeks. We have faculty meetings, curriculum to plan…" Her voice drifted off, as did her gaze, that seemed to be searching for that space on the horizon where heaven and earth meet, that place that Brice had taken her to. She pressed her fist to her mouth.

"I should have told him the truth in the beginning," she blurted out.

Alexis snatched a look at her as she drove, wishing for the hundredth time that she had not offered Naomi that piece of advice. At the time, she thought it was the best thing to do, a way to break Naomi out of her shell, free her from the constraints that she constantly put on herself. And it had totally backfired.

"Nay, I'm sorry. I should have known better than to try to make you into me."

Naomi turned to her friend. "Lexi, I'm a grown woman. I made up my own mind. And I'm the one who will have to deal with it." She sighed heavily.

"But no matter what, I had the greatest time of my life." She offered a tight-lipped smile. "If I hadn't taken your advice, I don't think I would have ever met Brice, experience what I experienced with him. If anything, I should be thanking you."

"Do you really mean that?"

"Absolutely. Meeting Brice was the best thing that has happened to me in a very long time. He made me feel all woman again, from the inside out. And for that I will always hold him close to my heart. I never thought I would get close to feeling like that again after Trevor. And that hurt so badly that I cut myself off, tied my emotions up in a ball and tossed them aside. I substituted books and work and moving up the ranks for a loving, caring relationship because I was afraid of being hurt again. Brice reminded me just how good life can be, and that's what I'm going to keep with me. I'm going to give myself a chance."

"Oh, Nay, I am so glad to hear you say that." She pressed her hand to her chest. "I was feeling so awful."

"Don't."

"What if he calls?"

"I'm still wresting with that. I think its best that both of us just remember the fantasy. If I told him now that I'd been lying to him all along…that's no basis for a relationship. It would never be right. Besides," she said on a breath, "we live hundreds of miles apart. It could never work."

* * *

The next few weeks, as Naomi had predicted, were hectic at best. Every day was another meeting, planning and preparing for the opening day of classes. As professor of African-American Studies, Naomi truly loved her job. There was nothing like opening up and challenging the minds of her students about their magnificent ancestry, their place in the world. But her goal was to be dean, which would afford her what she truly wanted, the ability to oversee the entire department, bring the professors up to standard and overhaul the curriculum. There were several professors that had been there well beyond their usefulness and had become jaded and non-caring. That wasn't an educator. She wanted to see each and every classroom led by educators that were passionate about sharing knowledge and passionate about getting the best out of each student. She knew that her position about certain faculty members wasn't popular with everyone, but unless they went after and secured the best teachers, all the technology in the world wouldn't prepare these students to compete on their feet. That is where she could make a broad impact. But if Professor Lewis had his way, that would never happen.

Naomi draped her purse across her shoulder, then tucked a loose strand of hair back into the tight bun at the back of her head. Her navy blue suit was one of her favorites. It always gave her that professional, polished look that she strove for. She never wanted to give any of the males in administration or on the teaching level, the idea that she was anything but professional, there to do her job and nothing more—which was what caused the rift and ultimate animosity between her and Frank. Years earlier before she'd gained tenure, Frank asked her out for drinks after work. In her mind it was a harmless, friendly gesture of a colleague. Frank had a different agenda and wanted more than drinks. She put the brakes on it right then and there. But it didn't seem to stop him. He persisted—stopping her in the hallway to drum up inane conversation, tossing out sexual innuendoes of how great they would be together until finally she had to threaten to go to the President of the college if he didn't back off. She'd learned to ignore him for the most part. He was more annoying than anything else. Frank would have loved to circumvent the college directive against relationships between faculty and faculty, and faculty and students.

Even if there hadn't been a rule in place, Frank Lewis was not her type. He was just as determined to win the dean's seat, and he had no qualms about making her life miserable in his quest to get it. Whatever he could do to stick it to her, he did—from undermining her in meetings, to withholding support of initiatives that she presented, even when he knew it was in the best interest of the school and the students.

That was the part of the job she was not looking forward to as she parked her Honda in her designated spot and crossed the parking lot to the entrance of Atlanta College.

She went straight to the main office and checked in, greeted her colleagues and plucked her mail from her box. She flipped through the contents and frowned when she didn't see her class grid. She approached the desk.

"Hi. I'm Dr. Clarke," she said to the administrative assistant behind the horseshoe divider. "I don't seem to have my class grid."

The young woman got up from her desk and came over to Naomi. "Yes, I'm sorry. We had problems with the computers, and some of the professors' programs and grids couldn't get printed out. They have someone working on it, and they say we should be up and running soon."

"Hmm, technology. Thanks. If mine comes up before class is over, can you send someone to bring it to me?"

"Absolutely, Dr. Clarke."

"I'm in lecture hall A-12." She thanked her again and headed down the corridor to her lecture hall.

The first day of classes was always chaotic. Students and teachers invariably wound up in the wrong place, or large classes were placed in small classrooms and small classes would be up in the lecture halls. She smiled and silently prayed to the education gods that her first day would be as free from disaster as possible, although she'd already encountered her first glitch. Hopefully, that would be it.

One highlight for her was that this semester she was teaching students who were in pursuit of their master's degree. That alone made them committed and focused. She was looking forward to challenging them intellectually and learning from them as well.

She turned the next corner and ran right into Frank Lewis.

"Naomi," he clasped her shoulders to settle her and then irreverently bussed her cheek as if they were really friends.

"Frank." She forced a smile. "Are you teaching this morning?"

"Yes, I am." His eyes rolled up and down her body. "Good to see you, Naomi."

"Have a good day, Frank." She hurried away, needing to get far away from him as quickly as possible. Her lecture hall was up ahead. She had about ten minutes before the students would start pouring in. That would give her time to get settled, sort through her handouts and quickly review her notes.

She pulled open one of the double doors and stepped in. She took a long, deep breath to settle herself. That first moment of entering a classroom always filled her with a sense of overwhelming duty and obligation. She was responsible for all of the young men and women who sat before her. She had the power to impart wisdom, to change and open minds. It was not something that she took lightly.

Slowly, she walked down the steps to the desk

below and put her materials on top, and before she knew it her new crop of students began to filter in.

Before long, the hundred-seat hall was more than halfway full and she began to wonder just how many more students she was going to have. She started to do a quick head count when her heart nearly stopped beating.

At the top of the stairs, heading down, looking for a vacant seat was Brice. But it couldn't be. That didn't make any sense. She was obviously imagining things. She swallowed, blew out air between parted lips to calm herself down. They say that we all have a double. This was obviously Brice's double. Yet, even declaring that to herself didn't help the shaking to subside.

Then he looked down and his eyes connected with hers. He stopped, frowned, took another step and stopped again, causing a young woman behind him to stumble into his back. When he turned to help her, Naomi took that instant to sit down, because she was certain that her knees were going to give out. She started shuffling papers on her desk. Her opening remarks had flown out of her head. Her fingers shook. The pulse pounding in her temples began to give her a blinding headache.

This didn't make sense. What was he doing here? She gripped the edge of the desk for support, and when she looked up the entire class was looking down at her, waiting for her to begin.

Naomi swallowed over the dryness in her throat,

slowly pushed herself to her feet and looked out onto the sea of expectant faces.

"Good morning. Welcome to Atlanta College. This is a master's class in African-American studies and literature. I hope you all are in the right class." She forced herself to smile at the smattering of laughter. "I'm Dr. Naomi Clarke. My students call me Prof, Doc, whichever works for you." More laughter. She smiled again and lifted her chin, gaining comfort and assurance in her element. "Let's begin."

Chapter 9

Brice sat through the forty-five-minute class in a stunned amazement that tap-danced between confusion and anger. At first he figured that the woman who could make passages sing, and who could breathe new life into arcane text, who captured and held nearly seventy-five bright minds in her hand *couldn't* be Naomi. Not the Naomi that he did things to that were just short of illegal. But of course it was her. This was the Naomi that he'd noticed the night she arrived at the hotel, with her corporate suit and librarian hairdo. Uptight Naomi.

Why did she lie to him? Why did she think it was so important not to tell him who she was? He was damn sure going to find out.

"I should have brought a tape recorder," the pretty young woman next to him whispered.

Brice turned slightly in his seat. "Hmm. Next time."

"I'm Pamela Phillips." She stretched her hand over her desk toward him.

"Brice Lawrence." He shook her hand, and when he returned his attention to the lecture, Naomi was staring right at him.

"Uh-oh," Pamela whispered under her breath. "Looks like we might have ticked off *Professor Doctor Clarke*."

Brice zeroed in on Naomi and rocked his jaw back and forth until Naomi turned her attention elsewhere.

"Well, that's it for today. Please review your notes and be ready to discuss author Chris Abani at our next session." She began gathering her papers, her gaze glued to her desk. She listened to the rise and fall of voices as they filed out and the door opened and closed. If she waited long enough, they would all be gone. She didn't have another class until late afternoon. That would give her some time to think. This couldn't be…

"Naomi."

She drew in a sharp breath and looked right into Alexis's eyes. She couldn't have been more happy to see anyone in her life. She nearly wept.

"What's wrong? You're sweating, and it's like an icebox in here."

She grabbed Alexis's arm. "He's here, Lexi."

Alexis looked around the empty hall. "Who?"

"Brice. Brice Lawrence. He's a student in my class."

Alexis chuckled. "Stop playing."

"Do you think I would kid you about something like that?" she hissed, her voice rising in hysteria.

"I don't know. You might. What the hell is he doing in your class? Didn't you say he lived in New York?"

"Yes." She bobbed her head up and down to reconvince herself.

"Well, damn, girl, if you were lying to him, maybe he was doing the same thing to you."

"But why?"

"How should I know? For the same crazy reason you did."

"Oh, God. This is awful. I can't have him in my class," she sputtered, jamming the last of her papers in her briefcase.

They started for the stairs leading to the exit.

Naomi stopped and grabbed Alexis's arm. "What if he's in the hallway waiting for me?"

"What if he is? You can't stay in here forever. Act like he must be mistaken if he says anything."

"Oh, God," she groaned again, suddenly feeling sick to her stomach. "I need some air."

"Come on." Alexis pushed open the doors and they stepped out into the rush of students and teachers darting to classes. "Do you see him?" Alexis asked softly as they walked toward the building's exit.

"No." Naomi's eyes darted up and down the hall, and she felt like a hunted rabbit. "I don't see him."

"Girl, are you sure it was him? Maybe your imagination is on overdrive."

She shook her head. "I…I'd swear it was him." Her voice faltered. "But…maybe I was wrong."

"Is his name on the grid?"

"That's just it. When I went to pick mine up this morning it wasn't ready. Computer issues."

"Let's settle this once and for all." Alexis took Naomi's arm and steered her back the other way, toward the administrative offices.

They walked arm in arm to Naomi's mailbox. Inside was a manila envelope. Alexis pulled it out and handed it to Naomi. "Open it and let's settle this once and for all."

"What if his name is here?" Panic shook her voice "What then?"

"We'll deal with that when we get to it." She waved the envelope in front of Naomi's face.

Naomi snatched it from her fingertips, turned it over and unfastened the metal clasp. She pulled the sheets of paper out and they rattled in her hand. The first page was a listing of all the faculty, along with their cell numbers and office hours. The next was her class schedule. The final sheet was the listing of her students according to section. She flipped through the pages until she reached the masters class on Monday.

Her eyes raced down the page then hiccupped to a stop when she saw his name. "Brice Lawrence."

"Oh, no, oh, no," she moaned, catching the attention of one of her colleagues.

"My sentiments exactly," she said.

"Come on," Alexis whispered. "Let's go outside, away from prying ears."

They left the building and walked around back to one of their favorite spots beneath a giant willow tree. With every step they took, Naomi was prepared for Brice to jump out from behind a tree or a building and demand to know what kind of game she was playing, although she could very well ask him the same thing.

They sat down on the wood-and-stone bench, placing their briefcases at their feet.

Naomi draped her arms across her thighs and lowered her head. "What am I going to do?"

Alexis put a comforting hand on Naomi's back. But she didn't have a clue.

Brice tried to pay attention to what Pamela was saying, something about her political science class and her internship at the White House the previous summer. He caught snatches of her diatribe, enough to keep up with the ebb and flow of the conversation. He wasn't even quite sure how they'd wound up bound at the hip and facing each other across a cafeteria table, sipping Snapples and crunching potato chips. He was still in a mild state of shock.

"What's your major?" Pamela asked.

Brice blinked her back into focus. "History. Yours?"

"Poli-sci. I intend on running for office and working my way up."

Brice's dark eyes roamed the cafeteria, looking for any sign of Naomi. But what if he did see her? What was he going to do? He drew in a breath and exhaled, releasing the tension that had held his stomach captive for the past couple of hours. When he got his class assignment, never in his wildest imagination would he have connected Dr. N. Clarke with the Naomi who writhed and moaned in his arms—who did things with her inner walls that gave him a hard-on just thinking about it. No, that's not who he thought about when he saw the name of his professor on his schedule.

"Do you live on campus?"

"I'm actually staying with a friend until I find a place."

"I was having some friends over tonight just to decompress, catch up and relax. You're more than welcome. Great chance to meet some of the other students."

"Sure," he said absently.

"Great." She went into her bag and jotted down her number and address on a piece of paper and handed it to him. "Plug it into your iPhone or BlackBerry." She propped her head on her palm and looked at him. "Hmm, I think you're a BlackBerry man." She smiled.

"And you would be right." He tucked the paper into the top pocket of his polo shirt, then checked his watch. "Hey, listen, thanks for the good conversation and the invitation, but I have to run. I have a class in like five minutes, and I've got to find it first." He pushed up from his seat.

"Oh, hey, I'm sorry. I can tend to be long-winded." She got up as well. "What's your next class?"

"Early Beginnings. Some kind of modified anthropology class."

Her eyes widened. "Yeah. Great class. If you get Professor Morris, he will probably have you digging up the lobby for some ancient something that he's discovered. He is a riot. But he makes the class interesting."

Brice chuckled. "I'll let you know."

They walked out of the cafeteria together and parted at the door.

"My class is in the next building," Pamela said.

"I think I'm down the hall." He looked at his schedule.

"Let me take a look?"

He handed her the schedule. "Hmm. Okay, you need to go back down the corridor and take the elevator to the third floor. It's on the other side of the science lab. And you do have Professor Morris." She handed him back his schedule.

"I'll let him know that he came highly recom-mended."

"So, uh, hope I'll see you later this evening."

"I'll try to make it."

She smiled. "If not, I'll see you in class." She turned and walked toward the exit and Brice headed in the opposite direction.

"At some point we're going to have to talk," Naomi was saying as they reentered the building.

"Or you could just go on as if nothing hap-pened."

"But something did happen."

"Nay, did it occur to you that maybe for the time being he's being discreet? That maybe he's just as stunned as you are? He didn't make any effort to see you after class. He's probably rocked as well. It doesn't matter that he thought nothing of what happened between you two. He's probably trying to figure out what the hell is going on. Did you really want him to come up to you after class and start demanding answers?"

"I'm sure you're right. I hope so."

They stepped into the cool confines of the building.

"Okay, I have my freshman Sociology 101," she said with a wicked grin. Alexis was notorious for putting her freshman class through the wringer at the beginning of the semester. Separates the sprinters from the marathon runners she always said—those who had what it took to make it and those who didn't. "Then I'm finished for the day. Want to meet up after?"

"Sounds good. I'll meet you in the teachers' lounge."

"Perfect. And Nay…don't worry, it's going to be fine."

Naomi pressed her lips together into a tight line and walked off toward her class.

Brice stood in the corridor after his class was dismissed, and perused the long list of professors and the classes that they taught. According to what was posted, Naomi only taught on Monday and Wednesday. Monday was her masters classes and Wednesday was her freshman session. She had office hours on Tuesday and Thursday. *Friday must be the day she planned on how to mess with men's heads*, he thought, feeling himself begin to fume again.

How could she? What kind of woman did that make her? Did she live some sordid double life? And to think he'd been making himself crazy for the past few weeks since they last saw each other. He'd lost his phone in Cancún, along with her number and hundreds of others. But Naomi's was the only one he was concerned with. But he knew she would call him. She'd want to find out if he arrived safely, if he missed her as much as she missed him.

But he never heard from her. She never called. And when he returned to New York he scoured the

Internet and 411 to find the Greenlight Bookstore in
Florida. There wasn't one.

He figured that maybe he'd been mistaken in what
he thought he heard her say. But he had nothing else
to go on, and as the days turned to weeks and summer
ended, and not a word from her, he'd made up his
mind that it was no more than a vacation fling. The
last place he expected to find Naomi was standing
in front of him, teaching.

He wouldn't see her again for at least another
week, unless they ran into each other in the hallway.
And then what?

Chapter 10

Naomi somehow managed to get through the rest of the afternoon without running into Brice again, which made the whole incident seem like a figment of her imagination. But she knew better. She couldn't count the number of times she'd read and reread his name on her student roster and visualized his face when he'd spotted her at the head of the class.

"It was surreal," she was saying to Alexis over a glass of beer and nachos, their favorite after-work snack. She dipped her nacho into the bowl of salsa, brought it to her mouth and crunched. She shook her head slowly.

"I'm the last person you should be taking advice

from at this point, but I think you should just leave it alone."

"But what if he says something to someone?"

"It's his word against a respected, tenured professor. Look at you. You certainly don't look the type to have some fling with a strange man on a Caribbean island."

"You don't have to make it sound so awful."

"I'm sorry. That wasn't my intent. I'm just saying no one would believe it."

"Thanks," she said drolly.

Alexis shrugged. "So, other than that drama, how was the first day?"

They discussed their classes and their students, who they thought would make it until the end of the semester and which teachers they were surprised had returned for another year.

"I heard the trustees will be reviewing the list for the dean's seat," Alexis said.

Naomi nodded vigorously. "Yes, and I've put my name back in the hat." The coveted seat had opened two years earlier and Naomi was sure she would get it. It would have been the salve to heal her wounds after her breakup with Trevor. The demands would have dulled the ache. Instead they went with an outsider. That lasted up until the end of the Spring semester. He'd gone on to greener pastures. Naomi poured herself into her work and waited.

She leaned forward and lowered her voice. "Which is all the more reason why I can't risk some craziness from—" she looked around "—him. I want that position. I've waited, I've worked and I've put in my time," she said, punctuating each word with a stab of her finger on the table.

"Honey, if it were up to me, you'd be a shoo-in. From what I understand, your only major contender is Frank."

"Hmm. I can handle Frank. I just remain polite and stay out of his way." She reached for another nacho.

"And I would suggest that's the best way to handle your Caribbean tryst, too."

Every time Naomi set foot on the campus, her senses were on high alert. By some miracle or divine intervention, she didn't see Brice for the rest of the week. Maybe he'd dropped out. Maybe it was some weird *Twilight Zone* thing and nothing the previous week had ever really happened.

She tossed around a dozen scenarios throughout the rest of the week, the weekend and right up until she set foot back in her classroom on Monday morning—and looked up and saw him coming down those steps, chatting and smiling with that girl... *woman*. A burn settled in the center of her stomach and crawled up her throat. "If some people would stop socializing and take their seats, we could get started." She slammed her notebook down on the desk, surprising everyone.

There were a few murmurs and many curious

looks that passed between the students before every one was settled in their seats.

She folded her arms tightly in front of her and surveyed the class. She snatched up her roster from her desk.

"I may not always remember a name, but I don't forget faces." She zeroed in on Brice, then turned quickly away. "When I call your name, please raise your hand. And please be forewarned that wherever you are sitting now will be your seat for the duration of the semester. So if you have any plans of changing, now is the time." She looked around, waited a moment, and no one moved. "Good." She rattled the paper in front of her. "Allen, Nicole. Arthur, Timothy…"

She continued down the list, wondering which one was the pretty lady with the dreadlocks sitting next to Brice. His name was next. Her heart pounded. She could barely get the words out of her mouth. When she thought *Brice* she remembered calling out his name, screaming it in pleasure while he'd licked between her legs, whipping her into near hysteria, or dipping in and out of her with such slow, deliberate precision that she saw heaven.

The sound of shuffling papers and throat clearing snapped her out of her daydream. She blinked. Her face was on fire. She felt as if everyone could read her salacious thoughts. How long had she been back in Antigua with her legs wrapped around Brice's waist, she worried.

She drew in a breath. "Brice Lawrence." She pretended that she didn't know where to look until he raised his hand. She checked him off on the list and continued, eager to discover the name of his companion. "Pamela Phillips." She smiled brightly when her name was called, as if somehow they could be friends.

Naomi finished calling off the names and then began with the lesson and reading for the session. Her animated and very engaged students made the time go by far too quickly. Before she knew it they were walking out the door, and she knew she may not see Brice again for another week—and he didn't seem to give a damn.

Naomi sat down behind the desk and gathered her notes, placing them one by one in her briefcase. The lecture hall echoed the emptiness of the space and the center of her soul. She'd never been so confused or so miserable.

For the next three weeks, Naomi decided to play Brice's game. If he didn't know her, she didn't know him either, which was fine with her. But unfortunately for him, she had the upper hand. She knew she shouldn't care one way or the other who he talked to or socialized with. If he was otherwise occupied, then all the better for her. But just seeing him with Pamela unnerved her, threw her totally out of character. And she took it out on him.

"Mr. Lawrence, please read to the class the first

paragraph of your annotation for *Philadelphia Fire*."

The instant he began she cut him off, telling him to speak up, interrupting with questions. She thrilled at seeing that dark look flare up in his eyes—and then she relented. Other times, she would ignore him completely. He would raise his hand to answer a question and she would act as if she didn't see it; or, when he seemed unprepared she would call on him.

The cat and mouse game that they played was a tango, the dance of seduction. And each meeting, each coming together, each challenge that appear in their eyes, only inflamed their need and made them that much more desperate to have the fire extinguished. It was bound to combust.

About a month into the first semester, Naomi had all but fled from her class. Every time she'd looked across the room he was staring at her, almost daring her to look away. Every move he made she read as sexual, from picking up his pen and twirling it between his fingers to running his tongue across his lips, or smiling at a remark made by one of his classmates, or the way he sat in his seat with his legs wide, reminding her of what she once had.

She hurried down the hallway to her office. She needed to be alone, to have a moment to think. One thing was for certain—this game that they were playing couldn't continue. She could barely sleep at night. In the classroom, she had to force her mind to concentrate on the lesson and not on how hard her nipples were growing when their gazes connected, or how wet her panties got when he lifted his leg and draped his ankle across his thigh.

But what choice did she have? She had a class to teach, and the only one who seemed bothered by this entire rabbit hole that she'd fallen into was her. Brice seemed to care less.

The sharp knock on her door startled her, making her hit her knee on her desk when she jumped. She squeezed her eyes shut for a moment and let the pain wash through her.

"Yes," she snapped. "Come in." She turned sideways in her chair to rub her knee.

While the door was opening she was already giving her spiel. "My office hours are clearly marked. So this better be impor—"

Brice stepped in and closed the door behind him. Naomi gulped.

"Mr. Lawrence, my office hours are—"

"Save it, Naomi. I can read."

"What do you want?"

"You know perfectly well what I want." He turned the lock on the door and crossed the room, walked right around her desk and pulled her up from her seat. "I want the same thing you do," he rasped, his voice as hot as she felt.

She made a feeble attempt to pull away. He held her tighter. Pulled her closer.

"Tell me you don't want me to ride you the way you've been riding me for the past few weeks, and I'll walk out that door and never say another word."

She opened her mouth to speak, but it was only a sigh of desire that escaped and beckoned him to her mouth. He pulled her hard up against him, groaning at the feel of her again. His mouth captured hers and she was even sweeter than he remembered, sweeter than in his dreams. Their kiss was deep and so intense that it left them both weak with longing for each other.

There wasn't time to think, because if they did, Brice would have never pushed her skirt high above her hips; she would have never unzipped his jeans and cupped his bulging sex in her hands; he would have never unbuttoned her blouse, pushed her bra aside and feasted on her breasts; she wouldn't have stepped out of her panties, when he begged her to let him in, or wrapped her legs around him and let him push up in her against the wall, where her degrees hung.

No, none of that raw, hot, ravishing sex would have happened had they been thinking. But they weren't thinking, they were only wanting—each other.

And, lawd! It was so good that Naomi had to bite into Brice's shoulder to keep from screaming, and he had to bury his face against the wall and in the tumble of her hair that had come loose from its clip to keep from hollering.

So good that they forgot all about the weeks of

tension; so good that they forgot they weren't on a Caribbean island; so good that she forgot she was a professor and he was a student; so good that he didn't care why she'd lied to him; so good that the only thing that mattered was that they'd found each other again.

And that's what they thought, as Brice gripped her hips tight enough to leave the imprint of his fingertips, and pushed up so hard inside her that she came with such force that her limbs stiffened, her throat clenched and it took all of Brice's strength to hold on, with her bucking so wildly against his thrusts that it set off his own climax, that burst in a stream of long-overdue release.

They held on to each other in the suddenly awkward position, trying to breathe, to clear their heads and make sense of what they had just done.

Slowly, Brice pulled out and lowered Naomi's legs until her feet touched the floor. They both slid down until they were cuddled in a heap beside her desk.

He looked at her, her eyes brilliant, her lips thoroughly kissed, her exposed breasts rising and falling, and the words tumbled out of his mouth. "I thought I'd never see you again."

"Brice…"

"We'll make time to talk. We have to." He helped her to her feet. He fastened his pants and fixed his clothes while Naomi retrieved her panties and got herself together.

She suddenly felt like one of those teachers that

she'd read about, who have sex with their students. But this was different. Or was it? Oh, she couldn't think about it now! Not with the way she was still sizzling inside.

He lifted her chin. "You okay?"

She nodded. "You?"

"Now I am." He leaned down and kissed her. He grabbed a notepad from her desk and jotted down his number and the address where he was staying. He handed the paper to her. "When you're ready." He walked toward the door and unlocked it. He turned back to look at her. "I hope it's soon." He opened the door and walked out.

When the door closed, she realized she was shaking all over. She needed to get out of that room, distance herself from what just happened, so that she could think.

She smoothed her hair and checked her clothing. Confident that she didn't look as if she'd just had the greatest sex in her life up against her office wall, she collected her things and stepped out into the hallway.

The traffic in the hallway was thin, since most of the students were in class. She checked her watch. She had a few minutes. She darted off toward the ladies' room to freshen up, and came up short when she saw Brice at the end of the hallway with Pamela smiling into his face. He slightly angled his head in Naomi's direction, then turned back to his conversation with Pamela before they walked off together and disappeared around the next corner.

Tears of humiliation were hotter than fire and they burned Naomi's eyes, her cheeks and her heart.

Chapter 11

"You did what!" Alexis screeched, as Naomi paced in front of her across the wooden living room floor.

Naomi hadn't stopped crying since she'd shown up at Alexis's door. It took Alexis nearly a half hour to make out what Naomi was saying over her broken sobs, punctuated with curses and threats and out-and-out wailing. Now the unreal scenario had finally come together, and Alexis, never one for a loss of words, couldn't put a sentence together. Her friend, her dear, straitlaced, conservative, often nerdy brilliant friend had certifiably lost her mind.

Alexis pressed her face in her hands, then looked up at Naomi, who continued to pace and wail. Any second now, she expected Naomi to start gnashing her teeth and tearing out her hair.

"Nay!" She held up her hand. "Stop the damned pacing and sit down. We need to talk about this. If it ever gets out, you could lose your tenure, your job… grrr. What were you thinking?"

Naomi plopped down on the couch, snatched a tissue from the box on the table and blew her nose. Her eyes were swollen and red-rimmed, her face flushed as if she had a fever, her always-perfect bun hanging in a loose knot at the back of her neck.

Alexis filled Naomi's glass with wine. "Take some."

Naomi reached for the glass and gulped it down all at once. She leaned forward and took the bottle and refilled her glass, not offering any to Alexis. She flopped back against the couch, sniffed loudly and started in on her glass.

"Naomi, sweetie, why?" Alexis's gaze implored her friend to tell her where she had lost her mind so that they could go and get it.

Naomi slowly shook her head. "I…I don't know. It had been brewing like a…stew in a Crock-Pot. Every time he was in class, the tension, the heat, just kept popping back and forth between us. I'd ignore him, then I'd single him out. And that woman, Pamela— she was always next to him, touching his arm, smiling at him. It was making me nuts. I kept wondering if he was doing with her what he'd done with me. And as much as I didn't want him to acknowledge what went on between us, the jealous, jilted woman in me wanted him to. I wanted him to let me know that those two weeks in Antigua meant something to him, too. That it wasn't just me, and that I hadn't given myself to..." She covered her face and her strangled cry slipped between her fingers.

Alexis reached across the space and patted Naomi's knee. As much as she wanted to hug Naomi and tell her that everything was going to be all right, what her friend really needed was some straight talk—and as her friend, it was up to her to give it to her.

"Naomi, listen to me."

Reluctantly, Naomi lifted her head and looked through tear-filled eyes at her friend. "You don't have to say it. It was stupid and reckless." She sniffed. "Every time I think about it, I still can't believe I could have done something so incredibly dumb." She sniffed, reached for a tissue and dabbed at her swollen eyes. She balled the tissue up in her palm.

"Naomi, let's just forget that it was plain silly for a minute. What really has you upset is not so much what happened in your office, but the fact that you saw him right afterward with Pamela."

She looked at Alexis with an awakening in her eyes. "Yes. Exactly. And he looked at me as if he didn't see me."

Alexis pursed her lips and looked at her friend. "Nay, what did you expect him to do?"

Naomi frowned in confusion. "What do you mean?"

Alexis blew out a breath of frustration. "Naomi, you couldn't expect him to blow you kisses, or in any way acknowledge that anything went on between you two. You couldn't possibly expect that."

"No," she said slowly, turning the word into three syllables.

"Then he did the right thing. He acted the way he's always acted. And you may very well be reading something into it that isn't there. You'll never know until you talk to him. But this is really complicated, Naomi. I mean, he's a student, even if he is a grown man. I'm not sure how things can work out with the two of you, and you certainly can't play the jealous girlfriend routine. If anything, if there is a relationship with him and this Pamela, that's more conventional than what's going on between you and him."

"So what are you saying?"

"I'm saying…I don't know what I'm saying. Pass the wine."

For the next hour, they commiserated about everything from health care reform, pension, new shoes, to what they really wanted to talk about—men and sex.

"Was he really that good, Nay?"

Naomi looked at her with dewy eyes. "Yes," she said on a wine-laced breath. "Better than good." She leaned back. "But it was more than that. The toe-curling sex just made everything else better. He's smart, and funny and ambitious. And he wants to open a school for young boys. He's handsome and sexy. He makes me laugh. He makes me feel good about myself again. I didn't have to be brainy and overly smart. I could relax and simply enjoy being courted by a man." Her shoulders rose and fell. "What am I going to do?"

"Didn't you say he gave you his number?"

Naomi nodded.

"Why don't you call him?"

"I'd probably say something stupid. I've had one glass of wine too many."

"You're probably right. But you should call him in the morning. But don't listen to me. I haven't been giving the best advice lately."

"I've stumbled this far. What's a few more potholes?" She laughed then hiccupped. "No matter what happens, we can't go on like this. There has to be a line, some agreement." She sighed and looked at Alexis. "And then there's my job to consider."

Brice was stretched out on the couch in the one-bedroom apartment that he'd rented, waiting for the phone to ring. He'd been expecting to hear from Naomi all evening, but the call never came. He pushed himself up from the couch and padded out to the small efficiency kitchen. He pulled open the refrigerator door and took out a bottle of beer, just as he heard his cell phone ringing in the next room.

He quickly retraced his steps and snatched the phone up from the table next to the couch. It wasn't Naomi.

"Hey, Carl," he said.

"You could sound a little happier to hear from me. Bad time?"

"Naw." He plopped back down on the couch and twisted the cap off the beer. He put his bare feet up on the coffee table. "Whatsup?"

"You tell me. You fell off the grid these past few weeks. What's going on?"

He made a sound in his throat. "You wouldn't believe it if I told you."

"That good, huh? I got some time."

Brice blew out a breath, took a long swallow of his beer and launched into his story. Carl knew all about the great woman that he met in Antigua. It was all that he talked about in Cancún, that and the fact that he was making himself crazy because he'd lost his phone. What totally blew him away, however, was the fact that the dream-come-true woman was a professor at the college—and *his* professor.

"Wait, wait, wait! Back up. I thought you said she was a bookseller, or librarian or something."

"Yeah, that's what she told me."

"Why?"

"Do I know!?"

"Okay, take it easy. I'm just asking. Have you talked to her?"

The steamy session earlier that afternoon in her office flashed through his head. "Not exactly."

"What does that mean? Either you did or you didn't."

Brice told him about their first meeting, the ensuing

atmosphere in class leading up to the sexcapade in her office.

"What!" Carl blurted out. "Are you crazy? What if someone would have walked in? Damn, man."

"Look, the door was locked and I don't need a lecture. I know. It just…happened."

"It just happened…?" Carl paused for a moment. "So now what? You haven't really had a conversation with this woman. You have no idea what her agenda is, and quite frankly, you don't know a damned thing about her. Everything that she told you in Antigua is obviously a lie. What else is she lying about? Maybe she's married or has a man. You don't know."

"I don't believe that." He shook his head in denial. "She's not like that."

"Are you listening to yourself? You don't know what she's like, other than the fact that she has you sprung, my brother."

Brice leaned back against the cushion of the worn couch. He knew Carl was right, at least a little bit. He didn't know her in the traditional sense, but he *knew* her. Deep in his soul he knew that Naomi Clarke was a wonderful, intelligent, sexy, extraordinary woman. And maybe a lot of what happened between them in Antigua was an illusion, but what happened when they saw each other again was not.

It was more than sex. There was a connection between them, a vibe that was inexplicable. All he knew was that he wanted to find a way to make it work…somehow.

"Yo, listen, I'm sure she's wonderful and all that. But you have to remember why you took a sabbatical from school in the first place. You have an agenda of your own that will impact hundreds of kids. You were lucky to get in there at the last minute. Don't blow it by getting caught up in some college scandal. If I see you on the news, I want it to be with you standing in front of our school with a big smile on your face, not hiding behind your suit jacket on *E!*"

"I hear you, man. I hear you."

"You need to work this out, B. Stay away from her, man."

A vision of Naomi's smiling face, her command in the classroom, her laughter, her wit, her lush body connected with his ran through his mind.

"I can't."

Chapter 12

Naomi awoke with a splitting headache. She really wasn't a drinker, and wine definitely didn't agree with her. She tried to open her eyes, then groaned when the rays of the morning sun forced her to close them. Slowly, she turned on her side, away from the window, blinked several times, and the room finally drifted into focus. Soft café au lait colored walls, gleaming wood floors, an ivory leather chaise lounge tucked into a comfy corner beneath a swag lamp hanging seductively above it and a small stack of books below. A blooming fern graced the opposite corner. She frowned. Nothing looked familiar. Where was she?

With a bit of difficulty she sat up and squinted

against the light. Then it came to her. This was Alexis's guest room. They'd both had one drink too many and Alexis insisted that Naomi spend the night.

"Ohhh," she moaned, pressing her palm to her forehead. She glanced at the bedside clock. Seven a.m. Thank goodness she didn't have class or office hours today. And then, like an opened faucet, the prior day came rushing back. "Oh…my…God." She lowered her head and shook it. Brice. Her office. Pamela.

She put her feet on the floor and slowly stood. At least the room wasn't moving. In the chair by the window, Alexis had piled up some needed toiletries. Gingerly, Naomi gathered them up, left the bedroom and walked down the hallway to the bathroom and turned on the shower.

About a half hour later she was beginning to feel human again. The pounding had been reduced to a mild, intermittent throb. Nothing that a couple of aspirin wouldn't cure. When she stepped out of the steamy bathroom she heard Alexis moving around downstairs, and went to seek her out.

"'Morning." Alexis greeted from her perch at the kitchen island counter. She was sipping a cup of coffee and reading the paper. "Coffee's hot, if you want some."

"Definitely." She walked over to the stove and poured a cup. "Any Sweet 'n Low?"

"Over your head, in the cabinet. How are you feeling?"

"Better." She grinned sheepishly, pouring two packs of sweetener in her coffee. She joined Alexis and sat down.

"I mean about what we talked about?"

"Better about that, too, actually. I'm going to call him." She took a sip of her coffee.

Alexis nodded. "Yeah, there's a lot of air to be cleared.

"Yes, there is."

Brice was tying up the laces of his sneakers preparing for a run, when his cell phone vibrated in the pocket of his sweatsuit pants. He dug it out and stopped short when he saw the number. *Pamela.*

Pam was a great woman. And under other circumstances he might even consider seeing where it could go. But she wasn't really his type, or maybe she was; but he was too fixated on Naomi to realize it. But the bottom line was Pam was beginning to make it clear that she wanted something more than to sit next to him in class and have inspiring discussions about black literature and the diaspora. She knew perfectly well that he was only there for the semester and that he was returning to New York.

"Hey, Pam. Good morning," he said, finally answering before the call got kicked to voice mail.

"Hi. Um, I know it's kind of early, but I don't have classes today and neither do you, and I was wondering if you wanted to hang out, maybe have lunch, catch a movie?"

A date. "Uh, that sounds nice, but unfortunately I have plans for today."

"Oh."

He could hear the disappointment in her voice and felt badly, but he didn't want to take this someplace it had no business going.

"Well, how about tomorrow?"

"Tomorrow?" He squeezed his eyes shut and tilted his head toward the ceiling. "Um, why don't I give you a call and let you know?"

"Sure. You have my number."

"Yes. I'll call you."

"Great. Well, have a good day."

"Yeah, you too." He disconnected the call and stuck the phone back in his pocket. He was really uncomfortable with the way things were going with Pam, and he didn't want to lead her on. He needed to find time to talk with her face-to-face so that there was no confusion, or worse, hurt feelings. That wasn't his style.

He turned off the air conditioner and headed out. He started down the tree-lined block at a slow jog and never noticed the car parked across the street from his apartment.

Naomi had been back in her house for about an hour. She could have stayed and hung out with Alexis as her friend suggested, but Naomi wanted some alone time. She needed a clear head when she called Brice, and she wouldn't get that with Alexis hovering in the background. For the past hour, she'd been walking back and forth with the phone in one hand and the slip of paper with Brice's number in the other. She stopped and sat down, stared at the number and the phone. She drew in a breath and pressed the numbers.

Her stomach began tilting and pitching as she listened to the phone ring on the other end. She gripped the phone in a moment of panic when she heard his voice on the other end.

"Naomi?"

"Hi," she whispered. "Um, if this is a bad time I can call back. Sounds like you're busy."

"No. No. This is fine." He grabbed the towel from around his neck and wiped the sweat from his face, then sat down on a grassy mound in the park. "I just finished my run," he said, still breathing a little heavy.

"Oh, look I can call back—"

"Naomi, it's fine. Really. I've been waiting for your call."

She released a soft breath of relief and curled up on the couch. "I, uh, guess I have a lot of explaining to do."

"Yeah, just a little," he teased. "And so do I. I'm sure the last person you expected to show up in your class was me."

"That's an understatement. I thought I was seeing things."

They laughed and the ball of tension bounced away.

"So, Ms. Mystery Lady, would you like to go first?"

"It's so silly, really…well…" She started from the beginning, from Alexis not being able to go, to her feeling totally out of her element to Alexis's brilliant idea to cast her real, uptight self aside and pretend to be someone else. And to her delight and surprise, when she'd finished her made-for-television tale, Brice burst into laughter.

"You have got to be kidding?" he said over his laughter. "It was that simple?"

"Crazy, right?"

"Yes, very. Woo." He wiped his face with his towel and then he sobered. "Was everything else make-believe, too?"

"No. No, it wasn't. And that's what made it so hard. I started off lying to you, and then everything got all tangled up and I wanted things to be different, but I didn't know what to do. And then, when I didn't hear from you, I thought it was just not meant to be anyway."

"I lost my phone the first day in Cancún."

"Oh, no."

"That's why I never called. I thought I would go crazy. I had no way to contact you, and when I got home I started looking for the bookstore in Florida and there wasn't one."

"Oops." She scrunched up her face.

"Thought it was pretty much a lost cause, and then there you were. And I couldn't put the pieces together—and you acted like you didn't know me."

"Oh, Brice, I'm so sorry for all of it. I didn't know what to do." She paused a moment. "Why are you in Atlanta, anyway? You told me you were a high school teacher."

"I am. I put in for a sabbatical because I'd applied for a fellowship. That's what I mentioned to you in Antigua, but I'd said I didn't want to talk about it just yet. When I got back home, all the paperwork for my fellowship and my sabbatical had been approved."

"Oh, my goodness. That is fabulous."

"Part of the criteria for my fellowship is to study the curriculum of several universities that teach African-American literature. My paper is going to help build the Af-Am studies department in the school that I intend to open. I wanted to gather the best teaching curriculum, in order to develop my own."

"I'm speechless. That is so incredible."

"Only the president of the school and the trustees know that I am a fellow. I want to keep it that way."

"I totally understand."

There was a quiet moment between them as they absorbed all the new information and tried to understand where this left them now.

"So, Ms. Lady, now that we've pulled all the sheets back, where does that leave you and me?"

"I was asking myself the same question. I wish it was something simple."

"Why can't it be?"

"There are university rules about teachers and students. I'm in line for the position of dean. If anyone ever found out…"

"I get it. I understand. But I also understand that there's no way that I'm *not* going to see you, get to know you better, make love to you. Not after all this. We have to figure something out, Naomi."

His clear, no-nonsense tone didn't leave her much room for argument; but as much as she wanted to be with him, she didn't see how she could make that happen without jeopardizing everything she'd ever worked for.

"We can't let anyone know," she suddenly blurted out. "No one. We can't be seen together. I don't even want you coming to my office." Her heart was thundering in her chest as she took this incredible leap into the abyss of the unknown with both feet and her eyes wide open.

"Whatever it takes, baby, whatever it takes. I'm not going to lose you again."

Naomi hugged herself as she listened to this pact that they were making. It was a risk. She knew it, and for reasons that defied explanation she was willing to take the risk.

"This is my address," she said. He scribbled it on a loose paper.

"I'll fix dinner. Around seven."

"I'll be there."

Naomi disconnected the call and fell back against the pillows of the couch. She leaned her head back and closed her eyes. Her first thought was: what had she done? Her second was: what was she going to fix for dinner?

Chapter 13

"Well, did you call him?" Alexis asked over the phone.

Naomi was puttering around in the black and white, stainless steel kitchen, putting the finishing touches on the sweet-and-sour chicken and checking the pot of steamed vegetables. She had this one room totally redone when she'd moved in. All of her life she'd wanted a Martha Stewart kitchen, complete with every pot, pan, and utensil that one cook could ever need. She'd had a wall knocked out to accommodate glass-enclosed pantry, the view providing the onlooker a visionary wonderland of spices, fresh herbs, condiments, pastas and sauces.

"Yes, I called him," she said, holding the phone between her ear and shoulder as she worked.

"And?"

"And we talked. I told him everything and he told me everything."

"And?"

"And we…worked it out."

"Nay, why in the hell are you being so evasive? What is going on?" She waited a beat. "You plan to keep seeing him, don't you? Naomi?"

"Lexi, listen, for all of our sake, just let it go, okay?"

"Naomi, listen to me. Don't do this. It could ruin you. What about all the years, the hard work? Is it worth losing for this man?"

"I can't talk to you about this any more, Lexi. I've made up my mind."

"I see." She paused. "You're crazy, you know."

"Probably."

"I hope it's worth it, sweetie."

"Me, too."

At ten minutes to seven, Naomi's front doorbell rang. She took a quick look around the kitchen, darted to the front, fluffed a pillow on her way to the door and checked her reflection in the hall mirror. She drew in a long, calming breath and pulled the door open.

"Trevor? What are you doing here?"

"Is that how you greet me after all this time?" His smile was broad. His deep dimples flashed. "I've left you messages. You've never returned any of my calls."

She tightened her mouth and folded her arms. "What do you want?"

"I came to see you."

"We don't have anything to say to each other. Shouldn't you be home with your wife, instead of standing on my doorstep?"

"It's over. Has been for a while. If you'd listened to my messages you would have known that." Trevor explained.

"Too bad that I don't care. Good night, Trevor. And don't come back." She started to push the door closed but he held it open with his arm.

"Look, I know what I did was wrong. I know I hurt you and you didn't deserve that. I've been living with that all these years. I made a big mistake, Naomi." He reached out to touch her and she jerked back.

"I don't know why you're here, but I'm not interested in whatever it is you have to say. So please leave."

He took a step back just as Brice's blue Ford Taurus pulled into Naomi's driveway. He turned toward the car. "Expecting company?"

Her pulse started racing. "That's really none of your business." *Don't get out,* she silently prayed. *Please.*

The car door opened. Brice stepped out and zeroed right in on the scene at the doorway. He slammed the door shut. Naomi prayed for the earth to open and swallow her up. He walked toward the three steps that led to the house. In the distance, Naomi heard the church bell chime seven. *At least he's punctual*, she thought despite her terror.

Brice was now on the top step with Trevor, and they were eye to eye. "Hey man, how you doing?" Brice stated more than asked.

Trevor stuck out his hand. "Trevor Lloyd."

"Brice Lawrence." Brice turned to Naomi and she saw all the questions hovering in his eyes.

"If you'll excuse me, Trevor." She stepped aside to let Brice pass. He stepped inside but not out of earshot.

Trevor leaned down toward Naomi and lowered his voice. "I thought that its only right to let you know that I was back in town." He paused, almost hesitant. "I want you back." He looked beyond her stricken expression to Brice, who was facing him. He waved. "Nice to meet you, brother."

"Yeah, you too."

Trevor turned to leave and Naomi shut the door behind him.

"Old friend?"

"Something like that." On wobbly legs, she crossed the floor and sat down in the arm chair.

"Anything I should know?"

She looked across at him. "Yes. We'll talk over dinner." She took his hand and led him to the small dining room.

"I'm not helpless, you know," he said, following her into the kitchen. "What can I do?"

When she turned to him he was stunned to find her eyes filled with tears. He went straight to her. "Naomi, what is it? Is it that guy?"

Tears slid down her cheeks. "I don't even know where to begin." She walked over to the kitchen table and pulled out a chair. She sat down and pinned her hands between her knees, her head bowed.

"Start wherever you want, and work your way around the rest."

"That was my ex," she said on a long sigh.

"I figured as much. What else?"

She wiped her eyes. "It ended two years ago," she began, and then slowly filled in the blanks, with the hurt and humiliation. How she'd turned inside herself and buried her needs and wants. "Until I met you," she whispered.

He took her hands and brought them to his lips. "He's a bastard for what he did to you." He squeezed her hands a little too tight as his anger grew. "How dare he show up here like nothing happened?" He jumped up from his seat and began to pace the floor of the neat black-and-white kitchen, running his hand across his head. He stopped and turned to her, his dark eyes hard and fixed. "What else?"

Her bottom lip trembled. "He said he wanted me back."

Brice reflexively kicked the leg of the table, rattling the contents on top. "Oh, really? That's not going to happen." He heaved in his anger. "Unless that's what you want."

She got up and went to him. "No! It's not what I want. That is over and done with. I just don't want him making trouble."

"What kind of trouble?"

"I thought I knew him once upon a time. I have no idea what he is capable of." She lowered her gaze, then looked at him. "He saw you. He knows your name."

"So?"

She shook her head to dispel the racing thoughts. Trevor tended to have a possessive streak when it suited him, she thought. If he figured someone had dibs on something he wanted there was no telling what he would do. "Forget it." She cupped his face in her hands and lifted up on the balls of her feet and kissed him softly on the mouth. "This was not how I planned our evening. And I'm not going to let Trevor Lloyd ruin it." She forced herself to smile.

Brice wrapped his arms around her waist and leaned back so that he could look at her fully. "That's better." He kissed her lightly. "Tonight is our night."

She rested her head against his chest and listened to the comforting sound of his heartbeat. She would put everything out of her mind except the night ahead with Brice. She had no idea what Trevor's plans were. The only thing she could be sure of about Trevor was that he was determined, and if he set his mind to do something he would get it done, no matter what it took, even if that included her. That was her fear.

Trevor circled Naomi's block four times. Each time he cruised by her house the car was still in the driveway. He didn't know whether to be pissed off or amused. He finally turned out his headlights and parked halfway down her street. He could still see the lights in her house from where he was parked.

He leaned back in his leather seat and thought about what had brought him here. He'd made some major mistakes in his life, and losing Naomi was one of the big ones. He thought what he wanted was power, prestige and the arm candy to go with it. He'd been so wrong. Melissa nearly ruined him financially and career-wise. When he'd discovered that she'd been emptying their bank account to take care of her lover he nearly lost it. He'd gone to the bank to have it out with his loan officer after receiving a letter from the mortgage company that he was in default. Obviously it was a mistake. After nearly tearing off the bank manager's head, he was taken into the office and shown the screen where his six figure bank account was displaying big fat zeros. Shaken, furious and confused he confronted her when she returned from her weekend away, supposedly with her girls, only to have her boldly confess that she'd been seeing Paul since right after their honeymoon. Paul her ex! He couldn't believe what he was hearing. It was a mistake to marry you, she was saying. She wanted out. She was packing and leaving.

He'd gone on a drinking binge, started missing classes, messing up reports and evaluations. Morehouse had no choice but to let him go. When the marshal came and padlocked his house he knew he'd hit rock bottom. He checked himself into rehab and hoped at some point he could salvage his career. So he'd come back hoping to find a way to start over, but it seemed like Naomi already had.

The downstairs lights went out. He sat up in his seat. He saw movement in her bedroom window, then those lights went out, too. He slammed his fist against the steering wheel, took one last look, put the car in gear and tore away from the curb.

Chapter 14

"Ooooh, yes…right there, right there…." Naomi cried. She gripped his back and raised her legs higher.

Brice swore he'd just dipped deeper into eternity. "I know, baby," he moaned in her ear, moving in long penetration strokes, in and out of her, grinding his pelvis against her so that he teased her throbbing bud each time he moved. He cupped her breast in one hand, its silky lushness overflowing as he massaged it and tweeked her nipple between his fingertips.

Making love with Naomi was taking a ride to heaven. He'd had women in his life that knew all kinds of tricks and could make their vaginas sing the national anthem, but none of them turned him out and turned him on like Naomi. He couldn't get enough of her. And the turn-on wasn't the sex itself, he thought, through a cloud of ecstasy, as a shot of euphoric pleasure shimmied through him when she twisted her hips and offered up her other breast for him to feast on. It was all that came before it—the talking, the laughter, the getting inside each other's head, the knowing what the other was thinking, anticipating their wants.

This—this was just plain old crazy, scramble-your-mind loving. The icing on the cake.

Her insides tightened around him and he gasped in shocked pleasure.

"Careful," he warned thickly.

She grinned and did it again.

The sound that rose from his throat was animal-like, primitive. She did it again. Squeezed and released in rapid succession until she felt his body shudder, his penis lengthen even further and fill to bursting, and she knew he was right there and she was there with him.

He dove his hands under her hips and pulled her hard and fast up against his demanding thrust. Faster. Harder. Faster. They were both caught up in the inescapable maelstrom of their desire for release, pushing each other to the limit. And then he hit it— that spot deep inside her walls—and she screamed for mercy as her climax gripped her in a viselike hold and shook her and shook her. And Brice was right there to catch her and release the gush of his own joy.

"We can't keep this up," Naomi whispered hoarsely into the hot curve of Brice's throat.

He slid his hand down between her legs and tenderly stroked her. "Can't keep what up?" He slipped a finger into the wetness.

Her body jerked and she moaned. "We're…going to…be too weak…."

"I like how I get to be weak. How about you?"

She didn't think she had anything left, but she did. She felt it building as Brice fingered her every so slowly. Her hips arched and fell in rhythm with him. He lowered his head and skimmed the crest of her breast with his tongue, before taking the tender, sweet nipple into his mouth and drawing it in. She clawed the sheets. He slid in another finger; and when her body adjusted, he put in another and she started to see stars explode behind her eyelids.

She knew it was pointless to fight it and she didn't want to. She spread her thighs and bent her knees, giving him full access and her unspeakable pleasure. And then he took her just where he wanted her to go when he used his thumb to caress her clit, while his fingers danced in the wet well of her essence.

When Naomi opened her eyes her bedroom was pitch-black except for the illumination of the streetlights beyond her window.

Brice's arm was draped across her middle and her back was pressed against his chest, spoon fashion.

She brought his hand up to her lips and tenderly kissed his fingers, then held them to her cheek.

This was more than she could have ever hoped for. She was afraid of what she was feeling. It was strong. Strong enough to make her take risks and toss to the curb the man that she'd once been ready to walk down the aisle with.

It didn't make sense. This was how you felt about someone that you'd known for a while, dealt with on several levels. Yet she knew that Brice was meant for her. For all the craziness, they were meant to be together.

He moved against her. "Hey," he whispered.

"Hey," she said into the dark.

He nuzzled the back of her neck. "I'm falling in love with you, Naomi." He kissed the back of her neck. "Can you handle that?"

She flipped over, tried to see his eyes in the darkness.

"I…"

"Don't tell me you feel the same way," he said. "Just tell me if you can handle how I'm feeling you." He ran a finger down her center and stopped at her stomach.

Naomi clamored onto her knees and looked down at his hot, dark silhouette then draped her right leg across his waist until she straddled him. She took him at half-mast and brought him fully to life. She rose up and pressed the pulsing head against her throbbing opening then slowly lowered herself until he was buried inside her.

"Yes," she said with a strangled groan, "I can handle how you're feeling me."

Naomi was finishing up in the shower after banning Brice from entering. She'd taken a long, leisurely, steamy-hot shower, using her favorite body scrub. She felt featherlike and happy from the inside out. Her spirit was smiling and she hadn't felt this way in longer than she could remember.

They'd spent the entire weekend together, not leaving the house except to take a walk to the deli for some coffee. They talked and laughed, watched television, discussed the plans for his school, made love in every room of her house, dug out some old movies, popped popcorn and simply enjoyed each other.

As she dried off, she thought about what Brice had all but confessed to her the night before last. *He was falling in love with her.* That took a lot for a man to say, and she didn't take it lightly. If it had been anyone else, she would think that he was just pulling her stings. But not Brice. She knew him—as crazy as that sounded, she knew him. He was sincere, and that realization thrilled her.

She tied the towel around her body, opened the door and stepped out. She walked down the hall to her bedroom and stopped short when she heard Brice talking.

"I know. And I'm sorry. I should have called…"

She moved closer.

"Right. Look, we have to talk, Pam."

Naomi's neck jerked back. *Pam!* She pushed open the bedroom door, expecting to see guilt written all over his face. Instead he smiled warmly at her and beckoned her to him.

Wary, she came to him and he wrapped his arm around her. "Yes, we'll talk. I think there are some things we should clear up. Okay. Good. See you in class tomorrow." He disconnected the call and tossed it on the bed.

Naomi waited for him to explain.

Brice kissed the top of her head. "Hmm, you smell edible." He leaned down and nibbled her ear. She pulled away and crossed the room, sat down on the side of the bed.

"What's wrong?"

She snapped her head up at him. "You tell me."

He angled his head to the side and looked at her. "What did we promise each other, once we got all the mud out of the way?"

She huffed. "That we would be honest with each other."

"Exactly."

"Whatever you want to know I will tell you. You don't have to hedge or throw hints."

"Fine. What did Pam want?"

He came and sat down beside her and explained about her phone call two days earlier. "I don't want to lead her on. She's a wonderful woman, but I know she wants more than just friendship."

"You're a little late with that realization. I saw that from day one in class."

He frowned. "Really?"

She pursed her lips and shook her head. "Men! Yes, really." She stood up. "So what are you going to do?"

"I'm going to talk to her. Let her know we can be friends, but that's it." He pulled Naomi down onto his lap and tugged on the towel until it fell loose and pooled around her waist.

Reverently he touched her. So softly she could have only imagined it. And before she realized, it they were making slow, slow love.

There's always more water where the last shower came from, she thought, as he took her on another thrill ride.

Brice left Naomi's house late Sunday night. Neither of them wanted to be apart, but they both had classes the next day. Although they'd spent most of their time naked or barely clothed, and Naomi had tossed Brice's clothes in the washing machine, he still needed to get gear for class.

They stood at the door. "I'll give you a call when I get in," he said.

Naomi nodded, her insides aching as if he was leaving the country and not just driving twenty minutes away.

"Tomorrow will be the real test," he said.

She looked up at him.

"We'll have to see how good you are at not letting your class know how crazy you are about me," he teased, which earned him a halfhearted sock in the arm. He drew her close. "Or how crazy *I* am about *you*," he whispered, before giving her a final kiss goodbye.

Naomi watched from her steps until his car disappeared. She turned and went back inside. Shutting the door, she leaned against it for a moment, reliving her unbelievable weekend. And she wondered just how good she would be at hiding that she was slowly and steadily falling in love with Brice, too.

Brice dug around in his pocket for his key and let himself in. He'd been in the apartment for almost three months, and not until now did it feel so utterly empty.

He missed her already. Now that was crazy. He chuckled to himself. Yeah, he had it bad. He walked through the front room to the kitchen in search of something cool to drink. It might be fall everywhere else along the East Coast, but it was sizzling in "the ATL."

He took out the last bottle of Snapple Ice Tea, twisted off the cap and took a long, icy-cold swallow. He finished it off, tossed the bottle in the recycle can, turned out the lights and walked to the back to his bedroom. It was going to be a long night, he knew, as he started taking off his clothes and tossing them on a side chair. He took his cell phone from his pants pocket, then crawled under the cool sheets.

From the light of the cell phone, he pressed in Naomi's number. She answered on the second ring. They talked for almost an hour, until Naomi insisted that they both get some sleep.

"I'm still heading that way, woman," Brice said before they hung up.

"What way?"

"Falling…for *you*. Hard."

Her heart tumbled. "So am I."

And before he could respond, she'd hung up the phone. In the dark, she smiled with happiness and Brice did the same.

The sound of a car's engine punctuated the stillness of the night.

Chapter 15

Naomi and Alexis met in the teachers' lounge for coffee before classes began and found a little, quiet corner.

"Where have you been all weekend? I've been calling. Did you get any of my messages? And girl, you are *glowing*," Alexis said all in one breath.

Naomi's eyes darted around the room. "We'll talk later."

"Nay…" She lowered her voice. "You didn't? The whole weekend?"

Naomi nodded like a little kid who wanted to jump up and down and do the happy dance.

"Guurlll." Alexis shook her head.

"Chile." She fanned herself with her hand.

"No more Caribbean vacations for you without supervision. You have totally gotten beside your bad self."

Naomi giggled. "We'll talk later. Promise. Oh, and Trevor showed up on my doorstep."

"Say what!" she sputtered and nearly spilled her coffee. "What the hell did he want?"

"I'll tell you all about it later."

"Lunchtime. Our spot."

"Will do."

They exited the lounge and headed off in opposite directions, toward their classrooms.

Naomi knew that she was going to have to work very hard to keep her focus off of Brice and on the lesson. She'd gone over a variety of scenarios about how the morning would play out, but nothing could have prepared her for what happened.

Naomi walked in and greeted the smattering of students that were already seated, then gingerly descended the steps to the place the professors called "the pit" and put down her briefcase and purse. Students began flowing in and taking their seats.

Then, in a scene right out of her worst nightmare, Trevor was standing at the threshold, surveying the hall, calm as you please with his visitor's pass clipped to the lapel of his jacket. Her pulse went off at a gallop. She unbuttoned her jacket because the room had become suddenly close and hot.

He came down the steps, lifted his chin in her direction and took a seat in the last row, near the door.

What is he doing here? She knew she would only make things worse if she called him out. Her head started to pound. Then Brice walked in, trotted down the steps and took his seat, never giving her a glance.

Her eyes darted toward Trevor, who was squinting down in Brice's direction. Naomi looked away, focused on her notes for the class. She felt ill. Her stomach was rolling in waves. The queasiness rose upward to her throat and burned, until perspiration beaded her forehead.

She drew in long, slow breaths to stamp back the need to throw up all over her desk and really make a fool of herself. Instead, she sat down, something she rarely did during a class. But if she didn't, she was certain she would collapse.

When her gaze flitted around the room and landed for a moment on Brice's face, she could see the concern in his eyes. She had to get herself together.

"Good morning. I hope you all had a good weekend."

The door opened and Pamela came in, muttering her apologies as she took her seat next to Brice. She gave him a brief, tight smile and flipped open her textbook.

Maybe, if she wiggled her nose she could make this all go away. Unfortunately, she wasn't in a television sitcom. This was her life.

"I'd like to begin today with the reading of several

annotations on the assignment, and then we will discuss them. Ms. Harrington, why don't you begin?" Naomi settled in her seat.

Looking everywhere but at the two men who now inhabited her life, she managed to get through the longest forty-five minutes of her life. She waited until the students began to file out. She was hoping that Brice would blend with the crowd or go out the other door. Instead, he walked right next to where Trevor was still seated.

Trevor stood up, subtly cutting Brice off before he could leave.

As much as she wanted run up those steps and stop whatever was going to happen, she couldn't move. Trevor was saying something, but Brice didn't look like he responded. He pushed through the door and walked out.

There were only two more students left that were making their way out. Trevor came down the steps toward her.

Naomi began jamming her papers in her briefcase.

"I didn't know that you'd started entertaining your students at your house…at night."

She snapped her briefcase shut and glared up at him. "You don't know what you're talking about." She jerked her purse onto her shoulder.

"I know what I saw."

"I have a staff meeting. Excuse me." She brushed by him. He grabbed her arm. She stared down at the hand on her. Trevor splayed his fingers and let her go. "Leave me alone, Trevor," she said, before she started for the steps.

"Not that easy, Nay. I told you I came back for you."

"It's not going to happen." She practically ran out.

By the time she got on the other side of the door she was shaking all over. She couldn't think. She needed some air. She hurried down the hallway, through the main lobby and outside.

It was barely eleven and the heat was bearing down on everything in sight. Naomi crossed the lawn, the library, the state-of-the-art theater and continued on toward the faculty parking lot. She crossed the hot concrete to her car, opened the door and got in. She turned on the ignition and put the air conditioner on full blast, leaving the door open until the interior had cooled.

This was all getting out of hand. There was no telling what Trevor might do. He could go to the administration or the board of trustees. Of course, it would be his word against hers, she rationalized, but it would beg the question: why would he come all this way to lie?

She pulled the door shut and rested her head on the steering wheel. The sharp rapping on her window shot her up in her seat, as if she'd been stung by a bee. Her heart raced. She couldn't breathe.

She pressed the button to lower her window.

"Frank?" Could her day get any worse? Frank Lewis was the thorn in her side, the curdle in her milk, the mold on her bread.

"I saw you leaving the building. I came out to get some papers from my car and noticed you slumped over the wheel."

"I'm not slumped. I...have a headache."

"Can I get you anything? A pill? Some water?"

"Thanks. No. I'll be fine."

"Are you sure?"

"Positive." She moved to roll up her window.

"I thought I spotted Trevor Lloyd up in administration this morning."

She swallowed.

"Weren't you two an item at one point?"

"What's your point?"

He flicked his smooth, dark brows. "Just asking. I was surprised to see him here. I heard he was discussing teaching here next semester." He smiled. "Well, I hope you feel better." He turned and strode off.

Maybe she was having a heart attack. That must be the reason for the ache in her chest. She pressed her hand to her forehead. No, Trevor could not teach here. There wasn't room enough for the both of us. There were thousands of colleges around the country why come here?

Her cell phone chirped. It was a text from Alexis, wanting to know where she was. She texted her back and told her to meet her in the parking lot.

* * *

By the time Naomi finished bringing Alexis up to speed with what had transpired during the past three days, she'd given Alexis her headache.

Alexis sat opposite her friend, with her mouth open. "You got me this time, sis. I don't know what to say. You've gone and stirred up some kinds of hornets' nest." She shook her head. "What are you going to do? Trevor isn't generally the type that takes a simple get lost for an answer."

Naomi pinched her lips together. "I know."

"Just the idea of him coming here to teach…"

"Naomi, you need to do some real soul searching and find a way to nip this in the bud. You and Brice might be able to keep things under wraps, but if Trevor thinks he's on to something, he'll use it just to hurt you, Naomi, especially once he gets it through his head that you aren't taking him back."

"I know," she muttered. "That's what I'm afraid of."

Chapter 16

"So you're not interested in taking this any further than the classroom. Is that what you're telling me?" Pamela asked, her tone growing confrontational.

"Pam, I think you're great. I really do, but that's not where my head is right now."

They stood facing each other in the courtyard near the fountain, with campus activity swirling around them.

"You didn't say that the night of the party."

He frowned. "What did I say?"

She laughed nastily. "So now you don't remember."

"No, I don't."

She stared at him for a long moment. "It's

obviously not worth remembering." She turned, hoisted her knapsack up onto her right shoulder and walked away.

Brice stood rooted to the spot until she was out of sight. Even in the midst of the blazing heat he felt a chill. He walked across campus to his car. First Naomi's ex, now Pamela. He reached his car and his cell vibrated in his pocket. He pulled it out and checked the number.

"Naomi. Hey, is everything all right?"

"No, it isn't. We need to talk."

"Did something happen?"

"No, not yet. Listen, can you come by later this evening? I don't want to do this on the phone."

"Do this? Do what?"

"Please. Just come by later. After nine."

"Fine, I'll be there."

"Thank you." She disconnected the call.

Naomi put the phone down on her desk and picked up the letter that had been left for her in her in-box. The committee, along with the board of trustees, was meeting in three weeks to review the candidates for the position of dean. She was one of the candidates in consideration—along with Frank Lewis and *Trevor Lloyd*.

She must have read the letter at least fifty times and still couldn't believe it. She should have known that Trevor was back for bigger reasons than her. It simply did not occur to her that he would be after the dean's chair. The bigger question was how long had he been under consideration?

He'd seen Brice at her house. If it came down to it, he would find a way to use that against her. She knew that he would, and he'd sleep just fine at night.

Trevor knew how much she wanted that spot. They'd talked about it and planned for it while they were together. He knew it was her dream. Was he that evil, that self-centered that he would not only break her heart, but finally try to break her spirit as well?

She pushed up from her seat. She wasn't going down without a fight. She knew that Frank Lewis had no real love for her and would shake hands and grease palms, if he thought he could pull the rug out from under her. But he didn't have the kind of ammunition that Trevor now did.

She took the letter and stuck it in her purse, gathered her things and headed out. Somehow, she had to work this out. But what was she willing to sacrifice in the process?

Brice had always been a man of action. He was never one to wait for things to happen. And he worked hard at seeing beyond the immediate, exploring all of the possibilities. But all of that had been shot to hell since he met Naomi. He'd been on a runaway roller-coaster ride that kept picking up speed and picking up passengers. When it came to Naomi, he couldn't seem to get his head clear. He was operating on pure emotion—something that was entirely foreign to him.

What he needed to do was be proactive. He wanted
Naomi, and he wasn't going to let anything or anyone
interfere with that.

He turned the car around and headed back to the
campus.

After her talk with Alexis and some close self-
examination, she made up her mind. In a little more
than a month the semester would be over. Brice's
fellowship would come to an end and he'd return
to New York. Although they hadn't talked about it,
that was something that was always like an uninvited
guest in the room with them.

Neither of them had dealt with the reality that
this was all just temporary. But it was. She couldn't
ask him to give up his dream. And she knew that
he'd never ask her to give up hers. They were at a
crossroads—an impassable crossroads. And one of
them had to take a stand.

It should be her. As much as it would hurt her to
lose him, it would hurt worse watching him walk
away and build a life that didn't include her. She'd
been there, done that. Not again.

So when he came there later that night she would
tell him that it was over. Finished. They couldn't see
each other anymore.

Even thinking about it twisted her up inside. She
didn't know how she was going to get through the
next few weeks, with him sitting in front of her and

knowing that she could never kiss him again, lay with him again, laugh with him again.

She took out two steaks, mindlessly seasoned them and set them aside to marinate. She washed two large potatoes, brushed them with olive oil and wrapped them in foil before putting them in the oven to bake. Then she went upstairs and took a long, hot bath, hoping to soak away the weariness that had settled in her bones.

Brice sat in front of the television. The news played in the background. It was risky what he'd done, and it could still backfire. If Naomi found out…well, he didn't want to think about it. He believed he'd done the right thing, and when it was all said and done and the time was right, he hoped that Naomi would feel the same way.

He checked his watch. She'd said "after nine." It was nearly nine. He pushed up from the couch and reached for his cell phone with the intention of calling her to let her know he was on his way, when it buzzed in his hand.

"Hey, baby, I was just getting ready to call you. I—"

"Don't come here tonight, Brice."

"What? Why? Did something happen?"

"I don't know how else to say this but to just say it. We can't see each other anymore. Not after class, not at my place. We can't. It's over."

"Naomi, you can't be serious. Why are you doing this?"

"Because I have to," she said, struggling to keep the tremor out of her voice, even as the tears rolled down her cheeks.

"You're not making sense. Just out of the blue!"

"Please, don't make this harder than it already is. We knew it was going to have to end sometime."

"What?" He paced the floor, running his hand back and forth across his head, completely turned around by what she was saying. "Naomi, let me come over there. We need to talk."

"No, Brice. We're done. I'm…sorry. Goodbye."

"Naomi!" The dial tone hummed in his ear.

What the hell just happened?! He'd worked it out. At least he thought he had. What made her change her mind? She sounded so cold and distant, not the Naomi that he'd come to love. The word halted his steps. Slowly he sat down. He was in love with her. He'd danced around it, hinted at it, teased her with it. But the truth was that he was solidly, deeply in love with her, and she all but told him to go to hell. What was he supposed to do with that? How was he supposed to handle it?

He swiped his face with his hand, then got up and went in search of a beer. He tugged the refrigerator door open then kicked it closed when he didn't see what he was looking for.

Stalking to the front of the apartment, he grabbed

his keys from the table by the door and went out. He needed to drive, to clear his head.

"You did the right thing," Alexis said, stroking Naomi's back.

Her body shook with her sobs. "It doesn't feel like I did the right thing."

"I know, sweetie. It doesn't now, and I know it hurts, but you're going to be okay and so will he. And one day he may even thank you for it. It was a selfless and brave thing that you did."

Naomi looked up at her friend, tears clouding her vision. "I feel like something is broken inside."

Alexis pulled her close. "It's going to be okay. It will."

Naomi nodded her head against Alexis's shoulder.

"Come on, I'll help you clean up the kitchen and put everything away."

Naomi sighed and slowly stood up. They walked together to the kitchen and began putting food in plastic containers and the unused dishes back in the cabinets.

Her plan had been to talk to him over dinner. Explain why it couldn't work, that she knew that he'd be leaving soon to return to New York and that he needed to focus on his dream, not on trying to figure out how to run back and forth to Atlanta.

She'd talked it over with Alexis and she'd made up her mind about the position of dean. If she got it, fine; if not, that was fine, too. At the heart of her she was an educator, not an administrator. She could do more good in the classroom. But she'd been so single-minded and focused for so long that she'd lost perspective.

It took having Brice in her life to show her that there was so much more to life than a career. And the realization that she would soon lose him forced her to see that she needed to start living.

She sniffed back a new set of tears. Even if that meant without him. He would be fine. She knew the passion that teachers had. She had that same passion, and there was no way that she was going to hinder his, no matter how much it hurt.

Chapter 17

There were only six weeks left to the semester and they were the most difficult weeks of Naomi's life. Besides Trevor appearing at every turn, asking her out or wanting to "talk," to which she dismissed every advance, she had to look at Brice's icy gaze every time she set foot in the lecture hall. Being so close to him and knowing how deeply she'd hurt and disappointed him was unbearable.

She was off her teaching stride, and several of her students had come to her after classes to ask if she was all right. The students would have to ask her a question more than once before she would respond, and then her answers would be short and sometimes condescending. It was so unlike her, and she didn't know what to do about it. It got so bad that she received a note to see the chairman of the department.

She wasn't looking forward to it, especially with the board's decision on the horizon. But maybe she'd successfully sabotaged herself and she could no longer be concerned about someone else doing it for her.

She packed up her briefcase. The note read that she should come directly after her last class. She steeled herself and crossed the campus to the administrative offices. When she arrived at reception she was told to go right in and that the chairman was expecting her.

"Thanks," she murmured.

The receptionist offered a sympathetic smile, knowing that not much good ever came out of being summoned to the chairman's office.

Naomi tapped lightly on the door.

"Come in," he barked, as if she should have known better than to knock.

Naomi eased the door open and entered the inner sanctum of the chairman's office.

Chairman Fielding had more degrees than wall space. He was an international lecturer on African, Caribbean and African-American culture, with two doctorates in literature. He'd taught for twenty-five years and became chair of the department nearly a decade ago. He took his job—the charge of teaching and the teachers who taught in his department at his behest—seriously. He always reminded her of Thurgood Marshall, right down to the thick, black-framed glasses.

"Good afternoon, Dr. Fielding."

He barely looked up. "Please sit down."

She smoothed her skirt and did as she was instructed.

He swept his glasses from the bridge of his nose and set them on the desk next to a stack of textbooks and folders.

"How long have you been teaching at Atlanta College?"

"Almost ten years."

"I've been looking over your vitae. Impressive." He peered at her as if to get her into focus. "In all the time that you have been here, I've never received a complaint, until recently." He linked his thick fingers together on top of the desk.

She swallowed.

"Two of your students have asked to be transferred out of your class. Although it's a moot point at this time in the semester, it gave me great concern." He leaned forward. "Would you care to explain, Dr. Clarke?"

"I'm sure it's a misunderstanding of some sort. And I have always maintained an open policy with my students that they could come to me if there was a problem."

He flipped through some notes. "It appears that you've cancelled or simply have not shown up on several of your office days. Would you care to explain that?" He waited.

Naomi's thoughts were running in circles. Why didn't he just put her on the skewer, roast her and get it over with?

"I've had a lot on my mind lately, Dr. Fielding, and I've…allowed it to interfere with my class and my students. But I assure you, sir, the curriculum has not suffered."

"Dr. Clarke, it's more than the curriculum, it's more than what is between the pages of a book, or a discovery on a field trip. It is the mental connection that you make with your students, your ability to engage them, challenge them, open their minds. You can't do that, Dr. Clarke, when your body is in the class but your mind and your heart are elsewhere."

He leaned back in his seat. "Had this been earlier in the semester, I would seriously consider removing you. I hand-pick the professors for my department. And it's with great care and consideration that I do so, because I have very high expectations. And I expect my professors to deliver. And when they can't…" he waved his hand in the air. "Then it's time for them to be someone else's concern." He paused. "Do I make myself clear, Dr. Clarke?"

"Yes, Dr. Fielding."

"Good." He lifted his glasses from the desk and put them back on and returned to whatever it was he was doing before she came in.

On shoestring legs, she managed to stand up. "Thank you, sir."

He didn't respond. Naomi drew in a breath, turned and walked out.

"You're lucky," the receptionist whispered. "He must like you. There's generally a lot of yelling." She waved goodbye as Naomi walked out into the corridor.

She walked straight to the water fountain and gulped down mouthfuls of water. She was actually shaking. By some fluke, she hadn't been fired. Well, they couldn't actually fire her, but they sure could transfer her to Siberia within the college, or make her life so miserable that she would leave on her own.

She ran some cold water on her hand and pressed it to her forehead, and then her throat.

"Why don't you let me do that sometimes?"

She spun around. Trevor was standing behind her.

"Go to hell, Trevor." She brushed by him, but he quickly fell in step next to her.

"You've been trying to get me to go there for a while, Nay, and it's not working."

"It's clear that they don't want you, either." She looked up at him and rolled her eyes, then doubled her step.

He chuckled. "Still have that sense of humor. It was one of the things I always loved about you."

She stopped short and turned to face him. "You

don't have a clue what love is, Trevor. You never have and you never will."

"You're wrong about that."

"I've been wrong about a lot of things when it comes to you, but that isn't one of them."

She started off again and he grabbed her arm and quickly let it go when he saw the fire flash in her eyes.

"Why won't you at least give me a chance, Naomi? I know I messed up. But give me a chance to make it up to you."

She looked him hard in the eyes. "I'm not that naive woman you left for Melissa two years ago. What you did to me took the blinders off. You hurt me so deep in my soul I didn't think anything could ever fill it, not work, not friends, not anything. But I found someone Trevor, someone who is genuine and cares for me. Who wants to make sure that I'm happy and cared for. I never did anything but love you," she said, trying to keep her voice from cracking with emotion. "It wasn't enough." She watched the truth jerk beneath his smooth skin, and his glance dart away under the weight of what he knew to be true.

"But I'm happy now. And I'm over you. So you can do whatever you want, try whatever you want. It doesn't matter. Trevor, the only person you're concerned with is yourself. You always have been. You didn't come back here for me. You came here because they kicked you out of Morehouse." His confident expression faltered like a stack of dominos that was beginning to fall. She chortled. "You didn't think I knew that, did you? You didn't think I knew that you were fudging reports and papers, and it all caught up with you?" She nodded her head as she watched the cavalier expression turn sheepish and ashamed.

"They may have tried to protect you by keeping it hush-hush, but I have friends, too." She blew out a breath. "Leave me alone, Trevor. Go on with your life and I'll go on with mine. I'm happy again and there's nothing you can ever do to hurt me. It's over. And if you ever cared about me as you claim you do, even a little bit, you'll leave me to my happiness." *Happy.* She wished it were true.

With that, she turned and walked away, leaving him standing there in a pool of his tarnished arrogance.

She had to pull her act together, and sticking it to Trevor the way she just did was the confidence boost that she'd needed.

She'd found out about his problems shortly after he turned up on her doorstep, during a casual conversation over drinks with a colleague of hers who taught undergrads at Morehouse.

Naomi never had any intention of using the information about Trevor, but he'd pushed her last button. She'd never even shared the information with Alexis. She promised her friend that she wouldn't breathe a word to anyone, and she hadn't—until now.

And in her mind, Trevor didn't count. She certainly wasn't telling him anything he didn't know.

She stepped outside into the balmy afternoon and glanced around at the sea of eager faces. She'd come here because she loved teaching. She loved sharing what she knew and it was time that she got back in the game.

Dr. Fielding was right. He didn't bring her into his department to take up space. And she wouldn't. Starting tomorrow, the old Naomi Clarke would be at the head of the class.

She crossed the campus to the parking lot and got in her car. She was going to go home, fix a light dinner, prepare her notes for the next day and do some real soul searching.

She pulled out of the lot, intent on her agenda, and never saw the car following behind her.

Chapter 18

Brice picked through his clothing, deciding what he was going to wear to the meeting, then packed them in his suitcase. He was glad that the investors that Carl had been working with were willing to meet late on Friday. That would give him time to prepare *and* finish up classes for the week.

Getting away for a couple of days would do him good. Since the blowout with Naomi, it had been pure torture to sit in her class, look at her, listen to her, know what you had, and realize that it was over. Over for reasons that she had yet to explain to him.

He jammed some socks in the suitcase. If she would have just given him a chance to explain what he'd done, maybe they would be together now. He closed the suitcase.

What did it matter? She'd made up her mind. Maybe she went back to her ex. Maybe the dean position took precedence. He didn't know. He didn't care. He walked past the dresser's mirror and caught his reflection. Who was he kidding? Of course he cared. Too much. He'd dreamed of her—at least on the nights that he could sleep, he heard her voice in crowds, smelled her scent. Sometimes her presence was so powerful that he'd turn in his bed at night and swear that she'd been there.

There had been so many times when he'd picked up the phone, dialed her number and cut off the call before it started to ring. He'd get up late at night and drive around the city, often finding himself in front of her door, looking up at her window.

Yeah, getting away would do him good. And in a few weeks this part of his fellowship would be over and he'd be back in New York, and maybe he could start putting this chapter of his life behind him.

He went to the kitchen and got a bottle of water. He leaned against the counter and took a long drink. He missed her. The idea burst in his head. Missed her so badly that it felt as if a part of him had been carved out and tossed away. How do you get over that? How do you ever feel better?

He'd never been in love before. Not real love. So this must be that heartache thing that he'd heard about and always tossed off as silly. It wasn't, and it hurt. And he needed to put an end to it once and for all, because he knew he couldn't keep living like this.

"You did what?" Alexis chuckled into the phone. "It's about time you told that a-hole off. Good for you."

"It did feel good," she admitted. She'd told Alexis about her encounter with Trevor, leaving out the part about Morehouse. A promise is a promise, she reminded herself, even though she'd been itching to share that tidbit of info with Alexis for a while.

"Long overdue," Alexis was saying.

"I know."

"So the good Doctor gave you a reprieve. You're lucky."

"That's what I keep telling myself. He made it clear that if it was earlier in the semester he would have kicked me out of the department."

"Hmm. Thank goodness for tenure, or he could kick you out of school."

"Believe me, I know I missed the bullet today. Well, I need to go over some notes for tomorrow and turn in early. I ordered Chinese for dinner. I wish they would hurry up. But in any event, I intend to do a Patti LaBelle and have a new attitude starting right now."

"Good for you. Well, I'll let you get to it. Lunch tomorrow?"

"Sure."

"Okay. Good night."

"Night."

Naomi put the phone down on the coffee table just as her bell rang.

"Coming," she called out, and went to get her purse. She went to open the door and the mouthwatering scent of sesame chicken and lo mein greeted her. "How much is that?" She took the plastic bag.

"Ten seventy-five."

She handed him a twenty, waited for her change, then gave him a dollar tip. "I hope I have my hot mustard in here," she said, peering down into the bag.

"Have enough for two?"

Her head jerked up. She hadn't seen him come up the walkway, but there he was standing at the bottom of the steps.

The delivery boy trotted down the stairs and back to his car.

"Brice…this isn't a good idea."

He came up one step and then another. "It's the best idea I've had in weeks."

Less than a foot separated them.

"I've missed you like crazy," he admitted. His eyes rolled up and down her face and settled on her eyes. "Tell me that you don't feel the same way and I'll turn around and go away." He waited.

"I can make it stretch for two."

He felt like a lottery winner.

She took his hand and closed the door behind them.

The moment was captured on camera.

"You went to the president of the college?" she asked, dumbfounded by what he had done.

"I wanted some clarity on the policy. I'd met the president some years ago and was reintroduced when I came here. He gave the impression that above all else he's fair and open-minded."

Naomi slowly chewed on a piece of chicken. "Go on."

"Well, I used a totally hypothetical situation, of course. And he promised to get back to me—and he did."

"What hypothetical situation?"

"Okay, what if a professor met a potential student, off-duty and off-campus, and they started dating, only to find out later what kind of situation they were in. And that the student wasn't really a student but a visiting fellow." He grinned. "That's when he shot me a look and his eyebrows rose."

Naomi giggled. "Go ahead. What did he finally tell you?"

"He said that visiting fellows were not considered matriculated students, and that although the scenario was highly irregular, there was no rule against it. He did warn me that 'whoever' this person was should still be discreet. No reason to cause talk, he said."

"That's what you were trying to tell me," she said, her voice laden with guilt.

"Yeah, but that's all water under the bridge now." He reached across the table and took her hand. His gaze caressed her. His thumb brushed lightly across her fingers.

The pieces to the broken puzzle of his life were beginning to come together again. That ache that sat in the center of his chest began to ease, and he could take deep breaths without hurting inside. This is what he had been missing.

He'd wanted to convince himself that he could move on, that he could push Naomi and what they had to the back of his mind. But he couldn't. And every day that he rose and slept, the purpose of it all escaping him, reconfirmed that inescapable fact: his life was empty without her.

Naomi lowered her eyes, tried to find the words to explain that, although what he'd done for them with the college was just short of heroic, she understood that the hurdle crossed was fine for their immediate reality, but what about when school ended and he went back to his life in New York and the rigors of getting his dream turned into reality. There were too many miles, too many demands that would separate them, make them resentful. She didn't want to see that happen between them. She wanted him to have his shot, and she didn't want to be the one that distracted him from it. He would come to resent her, and that was something she could not bear.

"Brice," she began softly. "I can't tell you how much it means to me what you did." She ran her tongue across her lips. "And for now that's fine. For the next few weeks that's fine. But then there is the rest of reality." She leaned forward, passion brimming in her eyes and her voice. She needed him to understand. "You have to go back to New York. You have to do everything within your power to make your dream of opening that school come true." She looked away for a moment. "You can't do that running back and forth to Atlanta. I can't leave and you can't stay."

"Oh, ye of little faith. You still don't get it yet, do you, baby?"

Her brows drew together. "Get what?"

He took a breath. "I'm in this for the long run. Not the sprint. I know things are going to be tough, but we're going to work it out. And if things fall into place the way I anticipate, we'll have much less to worry about than you think."

"What do you mean?"

"I'll know more after Friday, and I'll tell her everything, I promise." He took her hands and brought them to his lips. He placed a tender kiss on them. "I know what you were trying to do, Nay. You'd rather sacrifice us and your happiness so that I could have mine. But don't you understand, baby, that since you've been in my life, you have become that driving force. I could put up a million schools, reshape thousands of young, strong black men's lives, but at the end of the day I want you there."

Her heart was so full that it spilled over and slid down her eyes.

"Look at me," he said with a tenderness that was like a lullaby.

"I love you, Naomi. From the bottom of my soul, I love you. And whatever I need to do to make sure that every day that you walk this earth it's with me at your side, I'm going to find a way to make it happen."

The tears flowed so freely and so fast they clouded her vision, but she found his lips and kissed him with all the thanks and happiness and longing and passion that she had bottled up inside. He loved her. He loved her and she knew it was true and solid and forever.

And she told him. It poured from her lips and radiated from her body when they coupled and moved as one. She showed him by giving herself to him like she hadn't with anyone before. She bound them deep inside her body, hollowing out a place in her soul where they could always meet, no matter where they were in the world. And she whispered it in his ear, against his mouth, along the valley of his shoulder, with her fingertips, the rise and fall of her pelvis against his. She told him over and over again.

"I love you, Brice."

And he knew that no matter where he was in the world, this was home.

They spent most of the night snuggled together, talking in low whispers, as if they wanted to be sure that they'd shut out the world from their hopes and dreams and secrets.

Much too soon the sun was beginning to light up the sky and part the night like a theater curtain, offering the moon and the stars their final bow.

"I probably should be getting out of here," Brice said, although he hadn't moved an inch.

Naomi tightened her hold on his waist. "Hmm, not yet," she said, her voice still filled with intermittent sleep.

He kissed the top of her head. "Need to take care of a few things before I head out this afternoon."

"You sure you can't tell me?"

"I promise, I'll tell you everything the minute I get back."

She pouted then pushed up to a sitting position in bed. She brushed away the tangled mass of hair from her face and looked across at him. "Fine," she said, trying to sound put out. "Don't tell me."

Brice chuckled. "Oh, don't try the old wounded trick. It's not going to work." He reached around and pulled her down on the bed and quickly pinned her beneath him. "But this might," he said, his eyes darkening as he pushed her thighs apart and lifted her hips to meet the thrust of his entry. He groaned deep in his throat as he slid inside her, shoving the air out of Naomi's lungs so that it escaped in a gasp from her lips.

She lifted her knees and pressed them firmly

against his sides, holding him in place. And then they found their special rhythm….

More than an hour later, Naomi, thoroughly loved up and happily tired, leaned in her doorway kissing Brice goodbye.

"I'm going to miss you," she confessed.

He slid his hand between the folds of her robe and slowly caressed her, traveling downward to tease her one last time. She whimpered in delight before tugging his hand away.

"You'll never leave if you keep that up," she warned.

"Hmm, I know." He opened the door and he kissed her again. "I'll be back tomorrow morning. But I'll call you tonight." He pecked her on the lips again. "I love you.

"I love you, too."

He jogged down the steps and out into the already humid morning.

Naomi stood there for a moment and waved, as he backed out of the driveway, before going back inside.

The camera documented every move.

Chapter 19

Trevor had spent the past few days thinking about his life and the wrong turns that he'd taken. He'd made a lot of mistakes and hurt a lot of people along the way, mainly Naomi. It was true what she'd said about him not knowing anything about loving anyone other than himself.

He'd been so driven by his need to get to the top by any means necessary, it cost him his job and his reputation, at least among those who knew of the scandal.

He should have stayed up North when he left Morehouse, but something was pulling him back. It was the thought of Naomi and what they once had. He'd come back with the idealized notion that Naomi would be so happy to see him that she'd take him back and they could pick up where they'd left off.

He knew he didn't have much of a chance at the dean spot. Besides, he didn't deserve it. It was just another one of his games.

Why couldn't he simply be honest with her, without dressing it up in glib chatter and arrogance?

He put on his starched white shirt and began buttoning it. The truth was, it was all a facade. A way of protecting himself. If he put enough barriers up in front of him, nothing could get through. It was what he had done all of his life.

He selected a tie from the rack and slid it around the firm collar. He stood in front of the mirror and adjusted the tie until it was perfect.

It had been a simple revelation that forced him to look at who he had become. When Naomi let him know that she knew what he'd done, yet she wasn't threatening or even thinking about using it against him—something he would have done—it made him stop.

Even after all the pain and humiliation that he put her through, she was unwilling to become as despicable as he was, to stoop to his level.

He stared at his reflection, barely recognizing the image of the man in front of him. He wanted the old Trevor Lloyd back, the one with integrity and humanity. He hoped it wasn't too late.

Professor Frank Lewis locked his office door and returned to his high-backed leather chair. The manila folder was on his desk. It had been slipped under his door as per the arrangement. He turned the folder over and unfastened the metal clasp.

He pulled out several sheets of photocopied images along with even clearer photographed ones. It was obvious that some of these were taken with a cell phone. Those were the ones printed out on a copy machine. The others were from a high-speed camera.

But in both instances there was no doubt who one was looking at. Dr. Naomi Clarke and her secret lover, Brice Lawrence.

Frank chuckled as he looked at the images one after the other. They were damning. They were irrefutable. They were his ticket to the position of dean—a position that he deserved.

Naomi had been a thorn in his side for years. She gained tenure before him. She always landed the best schedule, her pick of classes. Her papers had been published in journals around the country and out of it. And he still struggled. It wasn't fair. He worked hard. He deserved to be recognized. And he would be.

These pictures would finally sink her. There was no way that the board would approve her for the position.

Frank chuckled and leaned back in his chair, spinning it around toward the window. Finally his day was coming. He tucked the photographs back in the envelope and stuck them in his briefcase. He got up, turned off the lights and walked out, happier than he had been in a long while.

"We did it, man, we pulled it off," Carl was saying, clapping Brice heartily on the back as they walked out of the Marriott Hotel restaurant.

"I know it's hard to believe. It's been a struggle. Almost ten years. But we're about to reap the rewards of our work."

"Now that we have the financing in place, we need to secure the location and a board."

"I know. I want to talk with you about that. I've been doing some research with all these classes that I've been taking and…"

Trevor was parked across the street from Naomi's house. He'd been sitting there for more than an hour, trying to get up the courage to cross the street and knock on her door. Every time the nerve welled up in him and he had his hand on the car door handle, something stopped him. Finally unable to stand his own cowardice, he got out and strode across the street before he changed his mind again.

He walked up the steps to the front door, took a deep breath and rang the bell.

He heard the bell echo inside the house. Moments later he heard footsteps and then Naomi's voice.

"Who is it?"

"It's Trevor. Please. I need to talk to you."

"Go away, Trevor," she shouted from the other side of the door. "I told you to leave me alone."

"Naomi, please. Okay, look I won't come in. You come out. Sit with me here on the steps. What harm could that do? Just give me ten minutes. That's all I ask, and I swear I'll go away."

Naomi peeked through the peephole. She pressed her fist to her mouth.

They would be outside. He wouldn't dare try to get cute in front of the neighbors.

She unlocked the door and opened it. "Talk," she said, then sat down on the top step.

"Thank you," he said, and sat down on the step below her.

Naomi folded her hands on top of her knees. "Well, I'm listening. You said ten minutes."

He lowered his head for a minute, trying to pull the words together that he'd been running through his head for hours, days.

"When we were together, I was afraid all the time."

"What are you talking about?"

"Just…listen," he said, holding up his hand. "I was afraid that one day you would wake up and realize that I wasn't who I was pretending to be."

"Really?" she said, the sarcasm dripping like sweat.

"I know I deserve that. But you have no idea what it's like being the other half of you."

She blinked in confusion. "What are you talking about?"

"Naomi, you have two doctorates, a tenured seat at a major black university, you're published in journals around the world, a sought after lecturer, you speak, what? Three different languages?" He shook his head threw up his hands. "And beyond being brilliant, you're beautiful inside and out." He lowered his head. "It was like, whenever I was with you, my own light would go out because yours was so bright."

"So it's my fault that you lied, that you cheated on me, that you married someone else?" She jumped up. "Please tell me that's not why you came here," she said, the fury burning her throat as she glared down at him.

"I came to tell you that everything that I did, the lies, the women, the marriage, even the scandal at Morehouse, was my own stupid way of empowering myself. It wasn't you, Nay." He stood up. "I wanted to blame you. I did blame you, because that was easier than admitting the truth.

"I wish I could go back and fix everything. But I can't. I wish there was some way that you could find it in your heart to forgive me for what I did." He breathed deeply. "In a perfect world, you'd take me back and we would find a way to make it work. But I know that's not going to happen. I do want you to be happy, Naomi, with whoever can bring that light to your eyes. I mean that."

Naomi listened, surprised and deeply moved. This

may have been the first time in all the years that she'd known Trevor that he was completely honest with her, showed her a part of himself that he kept hidden behind all the suave and swagger.

"Thank you for telling me," she said softly.

He nodded awkwardly. "I guess my ten minutes is up." He took a step down. "And about the dean thing. I applied months ago, never thinking that I would be considered, but I knew that whatever happened, it would give me a chance to see you again." He slid his hands into his pants pockets. "Well," he said on a long breath. "I'm completely out of confessions for today." He gave a lopsided smile.

"I'm sure everything will work out for you, Trevor. I do want that for you."

"Thanks. And I plan to let them know I'm out of the running on Monday. So you get in there and kick Lewis's butt, you hear me?" he said, wagging a finger at her before he turned and walked toward his car.

"Trevor, wait."

He stopped and turned. She ran toward him. She lifted up and kissed him lightly on the cheek. "Thank you," she said, looking him deep in the eyes. "I'm finally free inside."

He looked at her with the realization of loss and sadness, but with gratitude. "We both are."

Naomi went back inside and locked the door. Her world continued to spin at high speed. Had someone told her that Trevor would make that kind of confession, she would have told them they were crazy.

It was really sad, she thought, as she picked up some magazines from the coffee table and put them back in the rack, that Trevor felt so insecure about himself all those years, and that he caused so much havoc as a result of it.

But she needed to hear him say it, say it with truth and from the bottom of his heart. There had been a part of her that had felt inadequate, less of a woman, incapable because of what he had done to her—and all her brilliance, her degrees and education hadn't made up for it.

She turned out the lights and went upstairs. In a good kind of odd way, she felt herself and her world changing. And in celebration of this newness she was going to watch a reality television show!

Just as she was settling down and trying to figure out why anyone would take all kinds of abuse from a cook, her phone rang.

She popped up in bed. "Brice! Hey."

"Now that's the kind of greeting a man wants to hear from his woman. How are you?"

"I'm great, but missing you. I'm watching *Machete,* some kind of reality cooking show."

Brice broke up laughing, imagining his brainy, sexy other half attempting to make sense of reality television.

"Don't try to figure it out, just enjoy it."

She pointed the remote at the television and turned

it off. "Enough of that, what's going on? Where are you?" She folded her legs Indian style.

"About a half hour away from you. I managed to get on the late flight out on standby. Feel like some company?"

"Hmm, let me think about it. Yes! Of course. Did you eat?"

"Airplane food."

"No problem. I'll fix something."

"Humph, a woman who is fine, smart and can cook. Have mercy."

Naomi giggled in delight. "Just you worry about getting *your* fine self here."

"Before you know it. I have so much to tell you, baby. We need to celebrate."

"I can't wait. Hurry. Slowly. You know what I mean."

He chuckled. "Yes, I will quickly take my time. See you soon."

"Woo-hooo!" Naomi hopped down off the bed and twirled around in a circle in her bedroom, then hurried downstairs to put together something to eat.

Frank Lewis hung up the phone. A broad smile of smug satisfaction hung along his thick lips. The board had agreed to convene a special meeting to review the charges that he'd leveled against Naomi. It was simply a matter of time now, Frank realized. She would be out and he would be in. The way it was supposed to be. Finally, he could knock her off of her pedestal of superiority.

"Come on and eat, Frank," his sister, Martha, called out from the kitchen.

Frank pushed up from the overstuffed club chair in the den and went to the kitchen where his sister, brother in-law, Harvey, and his niece, Pamela, were already seated.

Chapter 20

When Brice arrived on Naomi's doorstep he couldn't wait to see her smiling face and hold her in his arms again. He felt as if he'd been gone a month instead of a day.

The minute she opened the door he knew something was wrong, even as she tried to force a smile and hold on to him as if she was afraid he would blow away. It wasn't an embrace of need, it was one of desperation.

He held her by the shoulders and looked into her eyes. "What is it?"

She swallowed over the dry tightness in her throat. "Come inside."

* * *

"They didn't tell you what it was about?" Brice asked as they faced each other across the table.

"Only that there had been allegations made against me, and apparently there were photographs."

"What?" he asked, alarmed in a whole new way. "Photographs?"

"That's what the chairman said. And they feel that it's serious enough to warrant a meeting with them, first thing Monday morning."

Brice's knight in shining armor gene kicked in and he immediately wanted to find some way to save her, to vanquish the villains that were trying to hurt her, then sweep her away to safety and happily ever after. But he didn't know where to begin. He didn't have enough information. But then he posed the question that was burning in the back of his head.

"I need you to really think, Nay."

She blinked rapidly and nodded.

"Is there anything, anything at all that you think could have been photographed and misconstrued in some way?"

She frowned, trying to think of what it could be. "I don't have a clue. I really don't." She shook her head in confusion. "I live such an ordinary, dull life of an academic. I go to work, I teach my classes and I come home." She looked at him and sighed. "I just don't know what it could be."

He squeezed her shoulder. "There's nothing we can do about anything now. So let's try to let it go, enjoy each other's company and the rest of the weekend. We'll deal with Monday when Monday gets here." He got up, bent down and kissed her forehead. "Come on, I could use a hot shower and some sexy company." He took her hand and gently pulled her to her feet.

She wrapped her arms around him and pressed her head to his chest. "I'm so glad you're home."

"So am I." He held her tight. "That's what I want to talk to you about."

She looked up at him and saw the mixture of sincerity and playfulness in his eyes. "Let's discuss it in a hot sudsy tub."

"I didn't want to lay it all out before we talked with the investors, but they have agreed to finance the opening of a charter school, based on the mission and criteria that Carl and I have devised."

"What! Oh, my goodness." She splashed water out of the tub scrambling to get to him. She squeezed his cheeks between her palms and kissed him sloppily on the lips. "That is so exciting. It's what you wanted. I'm so happy for you. Tell me everything. What's next?"

He grinned like a kid. "Well, we need to get a board of directors in place, start looking at teachers and location."

The light dimmed just a little in her eyes. This was the hard part, she knew, the part that she'd dreaded but knew was coming. She drew in a breath and put cheer in her voice. "Absolutely. How long do you think it will all take?"

"Months for each step. If we work it right and the stars align in our favor, maybe, just maybe we can open our doors in a year and a half. Maybe a year."

She nodded. "The main thing is that one big hurdle has been surmounted. The rest will be like rolling downhill."

"We want to make sure we do everything right, from start to finish. Actually," he said as he ran the loofah sponge gently across the crests of her breasts that bobbed above the water, "Carl is staying in a hotel in downtown Atlanta. He'll be here for the weekend before heading back to New York. I really want him to meet you."

"Of course. I'd love to. How about tomorrow? We can do brunch in the backyard. Or maybe you two manly men will want to barbecue." She grinned.

"See, now that's why I love you, you always know what to say."

"Is Carl single by any chance?"

"Yeah, why?"

"Hmm, maybe I'll invite Alexis, she's been dying to meet you."

"Do I hear a little matchmaker in your voice?"

"I'm happy," she said, leaning forward to kiss him. "And I want everyone to be happy." She reached down into the water through the bubbles and wrapped her hand around her prize. "Especially you," she said in a throat whisper, as she began to stroke him to heaven.

"What do you know about this guy?" Alexis whispered, while she and Naomi prepared the grilled chicken salad.

"One thing, he's fine. He's smart. He's Brice's best friend and I think he likes you. The rest you are going to have to find out for yourself."

Alexis put her hand on her well-endowed hip and looked askance at Naomi. "Somewhere, at some point when I wasn't looking, our roles got reversed," she said, bobbing her finger back and forth between them.

"What do you mean?" She added the diced cucumbers to the bowl.

"Once upon a time I was the one trying to find Mr. Right for you."

Naomi turned and smiled at her friend, then looked out the window at the men at the grill. "I guess I'm finally growing up and finding my way and myself." She inhaled deeply and turned back to Alexis. "I owe a lot of that to you."

"Me?"

"Yes. If you hadn't insisted that I go on the trip I would have never met Brice. I would still be living my same uneventful life, until you'd take me kicking and screaming to some club where I'd feel like a fish out of water." She paused. "It's not that way with

Brice. It…everything just feels right, he makes me feel right and good about myself, and it has nothing to do with how smart I am or what my connections can do for him. To Brice, it's all about me and my happiness."

Alexis looked at her friend in awed amazement. Right before her eyes, Naomi had grown up and struck out on her own. Bloomed like a plant that was finally given some sun. And Brice was definitely her sun. "So you think I might have a chance with Carl?"

"Is this *the* Alexis Montgomery talking? The man-eater asking *moi* what she should do?"

"Yes." She tugged on her bottom lip with her teeth. "I…want to get it right this time," she confessed.

"How about starting with just being your fabulous, funny, witty, genuine self?"

"You make it sound easy."

"It is. Once you pull back on the veils, being yourself is the easy part. Come on, I smell steak and I'm starved."

"Seems like Carl and your friend Alexis really hit it off," Brice was saying, as he smoothed Naomi's damp hair away from her face.

"I think she likes him."

"If it's any consolation, he likes her, too. He told me as much when I walked with him to his car. He wants to see her again."

"Really?"

"You sound doubtful."

"No…it's just that I'm wondering how all of that is going to work, with him in New York and Alexis here in Atlanta. Same problem we'll have," she said with an edge to her tone.

He pulled her close. "Why don't we not worry about that and let things work themselves out? It may not be as difficult as it seems."

"But—"

He cut her off. "Let me worry about it," he soothed. "I promise you, it will be fine."

She sighed deeply and relaxed against the comfort of his embrace. She'd let it go for now, but she knew at some point they were going to have to deal with the harsh reality of what would soon be a very long-distance relationship.

Chapter 21

Monday morning came much too soon. Naomi had barely slept throughout the night, and there hadn't been much that Brice could do to help the situation except to be there for her.

"I'll be right out in the quad, waiting for you," Brice said as they left her house.

She squeezed his hand. "Thank you. Hopefully, this is some crazy mix-up and it will all be over in a minute." But even as she said the words she didn't really believe them.

They came to a stop at the bottom of the stairs. Brice turned her toward him. "Just remember that no matter what, I love you, I'm in your corner and I will be there for you. Got that?"

She gave him a tight-lipped smile. "I love you, too."

"It's going to be fine. All of it. Trust me on that."

"Okay. I better get going. I don't want to add lateness to whatever they have on the table against me."

He kissed her lightly. "I'll see you in a couple of hours. Think positive." He waited until she was in her car and ready to pull away before he did the same. As he drove, he sincerely wished and hoped that the big pep talk that he'd given her would all be true.

Naomi sat in the reception office in the administrative wing of the campus. The walls were lined with the portraits of the college's past presidents, dating back to 1898 when the school was first founded by freed slaves. Atlanta College had a rich history, one which she taught in all of her freshman classes. She was proud to be a member of this talented and committed faculty. And it was something that she did not want to lose.

She glanced down and realized that she'd shredded the tissue that she had in her hand. She picked the pieces off her navy blue skirt suit and shoved them down into her purse.

The intercom on the secretary's desk buzzed. She picked up the phone, said a few words and hung up. She looked toward Naomi as she rose from her seat.

"If you'll follow me, Dr. Clarke, the board will see you now."

Naomi's heart was knocking so loudly that she was sure that the receptionist could hear it. She stopped in front of a heavy wooden door and knocked, turned the knob and opened the door for Naomi.

There were twelve men seated around the large conference table, and when she stepped beneath the threshold all eyes turned in her direction. Was this her jury, or the last supper? Her head spun with crazy thoughts

"Come in, Dr. Clarke," said Mr. Hastings, the chairman of the board of trustees.

Naomi stepped into the room and looked around. She wasn't surprised to see Frank Lewis sitting in a chair along the back wall, a smug look of satisfaction on his face.

She crossed the soundproof room with the intention of taking a seat in the back as well, when the chairman indicated a seat at the end of the table.

There was a knock and the door opened and Chairman Fielding walked in, gruffly greeted everyone and sat at the table with the others.

Something wasn't right, Naomi thought, as panic and confusion battled in her head.

"Now that everyone is here," Chairman Hastings began, "let's get this business started and finished." He bore in on Naomi. "Dr. Clarke, there have been allegations brought against you for impropriety by your colleague, Professor Lewis." He opened a folder and took out what looked like photos. He passed them down the table until they reached her.

She didn't realize she was holding her breath until her head started feeling light. She looked down at the pictures, not knowing what to expect.

Her heart stopped. They were pictures of her and Brice. With him in her driveway, kissing her, the two of them on the steps of her house, her looking lovingly up into his eyes.

She closed the folder and folded her hands on top of it.

"We've done some preliminary investigating, Dr. Clarke, and discovered, much to our dismay, that yes, this man in the photos with you is a student here. A blatant violation of this college's policy and a clear reason for dismissal."

She was about to interject and provide them with the information that Brice had given her, but decided to bide her time and see where this was going. If things went wrong, that would be her ace in the hole.

She couldn't see Frank from where she was sitting, but she could feel his smirk.

"However, it seems that several weeks ago Mr. Lawrence had a meeting with the president of the college." Naomi felt her insides smiling. She snatched a look in Frank's direction and saw the look of satisfaction begin to dissolve. "The president validated what only a few of us were aware of, that Mr. Lawrence is a fellow, and that visiting fellows are not, according to our charter, considered students."

Naomi wanted to leap up out of her seat, but she held herself in check.

"Therefore, the allegations of impropriety are dismissed," he continued. "Which brings us to a greater question and a bigger concern."

All eyes turned in Frank's direction. "Any faculty member that would stoop so low as to set out to photograph and—for lack of a better word—attempt to blackmail a fellow colleague is not worthy of working in this institution. We will be taking steps in the next few weeks to begin disciplinary actions against you, Professor Lewis. *And* your niece, Pamela Phillips."

Frank leaped up from his seat. "You can't do this! I brought you evidence. She doesn't deserve to be dean, I do!"

The door opened and two security guards came in. "Please escort Professor Lewis off the campus."

Naomi looked around the room as if she was waking from a dream. It was surreal as the members of the board gathered around her with apologies and well wishes. As they moved away one by one, she found herself alone with Chairman Fielding.

"Maybe now I understand a little better about what was going on with you."

She lowered her head a moment. "It was difficult."

"You are certainly an amazing young woman, Dr. Clarke. You have men from all corners either wanting to take you down or be your hero."

"What do you mean?"

"It seems that the other possible contender for Dean, Professor Lloyd, was the one who advised the board about Pamela's role and that she was Frank's niece."

She frowned in confusion. "Trevor Lloyd? You're kidding."

He chuckled. "Have a good day, Dr. Clarke." He walked out, leaving Naomi with her mouth open.

When she walked out of the conference room she didn't know what to do first, find Brice or find a way to thank Trevor.

She went downstairs to the main office to see if they'd set up a sub for her first class. They didn't, which meant that she had to be prepared to teach in twenty minutes. She smiled. The board knew all along how this was all going to go.

Naomi checked her mailbox and pulled out the plain white envelope. She frowned, turned it over and opened it. There was a handwritten letter inside.

Dear Naomi,
  I'm pretty sure that everything turned out fine for you and you're probably wondering

how I know about any of it. Let's just say, I still
have friends, too.

I must confess that I actually stumbled on
what was going on during the many nights I sat
outside of your door, trying to dig up the nerve
to ring the bell. (No, I wasn't stalking you.)
That's when I kept noticing the same car, and
the small flashes of light.

I decided to follow the driver one night, and
I couldn't have been more stunned to find out
that it was one of your students. The last time
I followed her she led me right to Professor
Lewis's front door, where he lives with his
sister.

I thought if I came to you, with all the
animosity between us, you'd think I was
lying. So I decided to handle it and I passed
the information along to the president, who
handed it to the board.

I'm not telling you all this because I want
your thanks. It is my way of somehow repaying
you for all the crap I tossed into your life. I
hope that it makes a difference.

By the time you get this letter I should be on
a plane to the West Coast. I'm really going to
start over and I have you to thank for that. I'm
going to stick with rehab (pretty sure you didn't
know about that) and try to build a life. And you
were right, I do owe you your happiness and I'm

glad that you've found it. Maybe one day you
can forgive me and tell me all about it.
You take care of yourself.
Always,
Trevor

Chapter 22

"Well, I'll be damned," Alexis said, chatting with Naomi a week later. "I still can't believe that Frank would stoop that low and then involve his niece. But what really blows me away is Trevor. Who would have thought it?"

"I know. It's been stranger than fiction, that's for sure."

"So now what?"

"Well, Frank will probably be dismissed. I have no idea what they will do with Pamela."

"I mean with you and Brice."

She drew in a breath. "The semester is all but over. He'll be going back to New York." She hunched her shoulders.

"And you're just going to shrug it off like that?"

"What else can I do? I can't make him stay here."

Alexis grinned like she knew something no one else did.

"Maybe you won't have to."

"What's that supposed to mean?'

"Ask your man. I asked mine," she teased.

"Lexi! What are you talking about?"

"Ta-ta, chica. We'll talk later." She disconnected the call.

Naomi tossed the cell phone on the table and pouted. She hated to be the last one to know, and it had been happening more and more lately. She shook her head. The last person that she expected to actually settle down was Alexis. She was Ms. Footloose. But since she met Carl she'd been a changed woman. She was calmer, more centered and genuinely happy. A good man could do that for you, she thought, as images of Brice came to mind. And now without the shadow of Trevor looming over her, and the craziness of Frank she could actually think about her and Brice and what was next for them.

She'd never been in a long-distance relationship and didn't see how they could work. It was too much stress and too much time spent apart, too much opportunity for things to go wrong and for someone else to step in and fill the empty hours.

But was she willing to simply let Brice go if they couldn't work something out? And what could that something possibly be, she worried, with her in Atlanta and him in New York? They both had careers and dreams. The more she thought about it, the deeper her spirits sunk.

Well, Brice was supposed to stop by. And he was not getting back out of her front door until she had all the information that she wanted.

Naomi cut a new path across her floor as she paced and waited and paced some more. She could not imagine what was taking him so long. He said six. It was already five minutes after six! She huffed—just as the doorbell rang.

She darted for the door, then slowed down. She didn't want to seem too anxious. With as much calm as she could summon, she opened the door. She put a smile on her face.

"Hey, baby," he crooned, sweeping her into his arms for a quick kiss.

"Hey baby yourself. You're late."

They walked inside. Naomi sat down on the couch, crossed her legs and her arms. "Alexis said you have something to tell me. And apparently she knows what it is and I don't," she blurted out without preamble.

Brice burst into laughter. "I told Carl not to say anything, but that Alexis has him wrapped around her little finger."

"Apparently, I can't say the same thing."

Brice grinned. "Aww, baby, don't feel that way," he teased, reaching for her.

She slapped away his hand. He came and sat next to her, draped his arm around her shoulder.

"What would you say to helping me open a charter school for young African-American boys here in Atlanta?"

She blinked back her surprise. "What? Me? Here in Atlanta?" Her heart was racing. "But I don't understand...I thought you were going back to New York."

"That was the original plan. I didn't want to get your hopes up before I was sure about the *new* plan. It makes more financial sense to open a school here. We looked at the alternatives, worked out all the possibilities and Atlanta made sense." He paused. "It would have had to make sense, because I can't see myself moving through life day-to-day without you, Naomi." He cupped her face in his hands. "I want you with me. I want your brilliant mind, I want your sexy body, I want your support, your guidance and your love. And in return, I promise to keep a smile on your face, stimulate your mind, challenge you to reach your goals. And I'll spend every day of my life loving you and making the world better with you at my side." His gazed dance over her face.

He reached in his pocket and took out a sparkling diamond ring.

"This is what took me so long. Marry me, Nay. Let's conquer the world together." He took her hand and held the ring, waiting for her response.

Through her tears of joy she looked upon the man

who had changed her life, made her look at the world and herself in a whole new way. Every day with Brice Lawrence was a new lesson in life, and she couldn't wait to start their next chapter.

"Yes, yes, yes…" she whispered against his waiting lips.

* * * * *

REQUEST YOUR FREE BOOKS!

2 FREE NOVELS
PLUS 2 FREE GIFTS!

KIMANI™
ROMANCE

Love's ultimate destination!

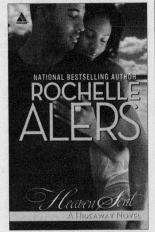

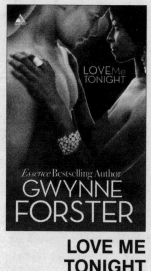

Silhouette Desire

New York Times and USA TODAY
bestselling author

BRENDA JACKSON

brings you

WHAT A WESTMORELAND WANTS,

another seductive Westmoreland tale.

MAN of the MONTH

Part of the Man of the Month series

Callum is hopeful that once he gets
Gemma Westmoreland on his native turf
he will wine and dine her with a seduction plan
he has been working on for years—one that
guarantees to make her his.

Available September wherever books are sold.

**Look for a new Man of the Month
by other top selling authors each month.**

Always Powerful, Passionate and Provocative.